## WITCHES' CHILDREN

"Narrated by the bound girl Mary Warren, the story tells how a little group of girls began to congregate at the home of Betty Parris, daughter of the stern Reverend Samuel Parris. Their imaginations stirred by the trances and the fortune-telling of the exotic slave Tituba, the girls soon fell into a contagious hysteria that quickly spread from the timid younger children to the bored, bolder adolescents....The girls became 'the pitied darlings of Salem Village' and were soon enjoying a heady power over the frightened, confused adults, pushing the frenzied madness to its catastrophic conclusion." —*Horn Book*

# WITCHES' CHILDREN
## A Story of Salem

Patricia Clapp

Puffin Books

PUFFIN BOOKS

Viking Penguin Inc., 40 West 23rd Street, New York, New York 10010, U.S.A.
Penguin Books Ltd, 27 Wrights Lane, London W8 5TZ (Publishing & Editorial) and
Harmondsworth, Middlesex, England (Distribution & Warehouse)
Penguin Books Australia Ltd, Ringwood, Victoria, Australia
Penguin Books Canada Limited, 2801 John Street, Markham, Ontario, Canada L3R 1B4
Penguin Books (N.Z.) Ltd, 182-190 Wairau Road, Auckland 10, New Zealand

First published by Lothrop, Lee & Shepard Books, 1982
Reprinted by arrangement with William Morrow and Company, Inc.
Published in Puffin Books 1987
Copyright © Patricia Clapp, 1982
All rights reserved
Printed in the United States of America by R. R. Donnelley & Sons Company,
Harrisonburg, Virginia
Set in Garamond Book

Library of Congress Cataloging-in-Publication Data
Clapp, Patricia.      Witches' children.
Reprint. Originally published: New York:
Lothrop, Lee & Shepard Books, 1982.
Summary: During the winter of 1692, when the young
girls of Salem suddenly find themselves subject to fits
of screaming and strange visions, some believe that they
have seen the devil and are the victims of witches.
1. Trials (Witchcraft)—Massachusetts—Salem—Juvenile
fiction.  [1. Witchcraft—Fiction.  2. Trials (Witchcraft)—Fiction.  3. Salem (Mass.)
History—Fiction]  I. Title.
[PZ7.C5294Wi  1987]    [Fic]    87-16507    ISBN 0-14-032407-0

*For my husband, Edward,*
*  and for our special ten—*
*Stacey, Julie, Andrew, Matt, and Amy,*
*Wendy, Jonathan, and Liza,*
*David and Jennifer—*
*          with love.*

# WITCHES' CHILDREN

# ONE

I WAS A LITTLE OLDER than most of them, old enough, as John Proctor said, "to have a little sense in your head!" If I was not strong enough to resist the madness, how could children as young as Betty Parris and her cousin, Abigail Williams, withstand it? Surely they were helpless. Betty was but nine and Abigail eleven. Or were they helpless? Were any of us? Did we in fact make it happen?

It all began so quietly! I remember an ice-covered January afternoon when I opened the door to the kitchen of the Parris house to find Betty curled on one of the settles, moping with some minor ailment. Abigail sat erect, ankles properly crossed, on the facing settle, and Tituba was on a stool between them.

Tituba! A slender woman, soft-voiced, dark-eyed—eyes so dark in her pale brown face that they sometimes glowed like coals. The Reverend Samuel Parris had brought Tituba and her husband, John Indian, back with him from Barbados five or six years before. Tituba, always quiet and gentle, cherished and coddled Betty Parris far more than her parents ever did. The people of Massachusetts Bay Colony believed that life was a stern, demanding experience, and that children must be made strong enough to endure it. Coddling was not their way.

Tituba. What did she see in her cards? What did she see in the palms of our hands? Did she, in truth, know spells and magic learned in that mysterious distant island of Barbados? Looking back, it seems she was but the spark that lit the willing tinder of our stifled, repressed young minds. Who will ever be sure? It may be that if I put some of these thoughts on paper it will all come clearer to me. Perhaps I can find some sort of answer for myself, for God knows that if I cannot find such an answer I shall end my days in helpless agony!

Back to the beginning then, that January of 1692, when Salem Village lay quiet beneath banked snow. I have never lived anywhere but Salem, so I know little of how life may be in other New England towns. A man named Roger Conant first settled here many years ago in 1626, calling the place by an Indian name, Naumkeag, and planning to make a thriving fishing village of it. Some few years later it served as the start of the Massachusetts Bay Colony when one John Winthrop arrived from England with a charter for land and a little group of people in search of religious freedom. It became Salem then, and its new inhabitants turned to farming and the enjoyment of that freedom they had sought, though how they could speak of "freedom" or "enjoyment" it is hard for me to understand, since there seemed little of either in the strictures the elders believed in and enforced. Perhaps it was irksome only to the young, with their natural high spirits, which we were told to spend on productive tasks for the good of the community.

I always tried to be obedient, but that year it seemed that winter had lasted for an eternity. There was not even the excitement and sociability of such gatherings as husking bees or house raisings with the ground hard frozen, and in Salem there were no Christmas festivities such as there were in Plymouth and its neighboring settlements. Men found indoor chores to do, carpentering and repairing and the like, but for females the work continued on its unchanging, grinding daily round with only church services to break the pattern. 'Tis said the Devil finds work for idle hands, but I believe he finds it for idle minds as well, for though my hands were rarely idle, my mind was often dulled and empty of stimulation.

My name is Mary Warren, and I was a bound girl to John and Elizabeth Proctor, who had taken me in some years before when my parents died from the smallpox that had come again to scourge Salem Village. It was not easy to be bound out. Such a girl had little to call her own. Even a daughter living with her family had scant position unless she had been spoken for by some man, and marriage was considered a most solemn bond, not to be entered into until a lass reached twenty years or more. Then, too, a girl might think twice did she note the lives of married women who spent their days in household toil and their years in child-bearing. Most likely, however, I would have settled for that had someone set his eyes favorably upon me, but there were at that time in Salem Village a great number of young girls and far too few young men to wed them. In any case, there I was with the Proctors, and I knew I should be grateful to them. I had a small room of my own, food to eat, sufficient modest clothing so I was always neat, and work enough to keep me busy from sunup to bedtime. But gratitude was not precisely what I felt.

John Proctor was a tall, strong, quiet man, for whom I had nothing but adoration. His wife, the gentle Elizabeth, was too sweet for my taste. I much preferred her husband's gruff commands to her soft requests. In my eyes John Proctor could do no wrong, and I worshiped him, blindly and secretly. The only other man I had known closely was my father, a stern, God-fearing soul who would have preferred several sturdy sons to one daughter. For Father the word *duty* replaced the word *love*. Now, in this somewhat warmer household, I found my healthy, eager, developing body responding to John Proctor's maleness. If he touched my shoulder in passing I thrilled. Whatever words he spoke to me I cherished, trying to believe they held more than the plain facts they stated. When he was within the house I pinched my cheeks often to bring color to my pale skin, and I brushed a damp finger upward on my lashes so they might better frame my eyes, always hoping he might notice the small green flecks deep in the brown. I would bite my lips to redden them and tighten the apron strings round my small waist until I nigh gasped. Ah, 'twas all vanity, and well I knew it even then, but young females are more given to feelings than to reason. In truth, I also knew that John Proctor saw naught that I wanted him to see. I was only Mary Warren, his bound girl.

It was Mistress Proctor, that bitter January afternoon, who asked me to carry a sack of potatoes to Reverend Parris's house, since it was custom for members of a congregation to augment a preacher's modest wage with foodstuffs and fuel for his fire. "And be sure to ask how Mistress Parris does, Mary, and say that I am deep concerned about her cough. And you may spend a short while with the girls, if you choose, but I shall need you home before sunset."

"Yes, ma'am," I said. Wrapped head to toe in every warm garment I possessed, I slipped and slid over the iced snow, teeth chattering, clutching the heavy sack of potatoes, to the neat small house where Samuel Parris lived with his wife, Elizabeth, his wife's niece, Abigail Williams, his daughter, Betty, and his slaves, Tituba and John Indian.

The door opened on warmth from the flames that frolicked in the great fireplace, silhouetting Tituba and the two girls. They turned to greet me as I entered.

"Potatoes," I said breathlessly, setting the heavy sack on the floor. I looked at the younger girl, huddled into a small quiet heap on the settle, her eyes wide as she gazed into the fire. "Is Betty ailing?" I asked.

"My Betty got herself a small 'gestion in her chest," Tituba said, smiling. "She be all right soon."

"Betty just likes to lie about and have Tituba fuss over her!" Abigail said in a high-pitched, fretful voice. "And surely there is naught else for any of us to do."

"There be aplenty to do," Tituba corrected. "That chicken to pluck so it can go in the pot with the carrots, and the potatoes Mary brought—"

"Oh, stuff!" Abigail thumped a small fist on the arm of the settle. "I have no love for plucking feathers off chickens! Come and sit down, Mary. Is it very cold outdoors?"

"'Tis frigid cold!" I unwound my several shawls and cloak and hung them on a wall peg, then sat down beside Abby, holding out my hands to the fire to warm them. "My fingers and toes seem made of ice!"

Tituba leaned down and slipped my shoes off, rubbing my woolen-stockinged feet in her slender hands.

"The fire soon warm you through," she said. "Betty, child, you want a drink of Tituba's herb tea? It help you feel better."

With a little sigh, Betty spoke. "No more tea, Tituba. I am full of tea!" Turning her dark eyes from the fire, she looked lovingly at Tituba. "But read my palm for me! Tell me what exciting things are going to happen to me!"

Tituba laughed softly. "Exciting things!" she echoed. "My Betty too young for excitements."

"She'll be an old, old woman before there is any excitement around here," Abigail said fretfully. "We all will! I don't think there has been a drop of excitement in Salem Village since it was settled!" She uncrossed her ankles and swung her legs vigorously. "There are times when I feel

14

like that jug of cider Uncle Samuel had that blew the bung from its neck and splashed the rafters!"

I laughed at Abigail's scowling face. "And what sort of excitement would you have?" I asked.

"How can I know? I have never known any! Oh, Tituba, read Betty's hand! Mayhap you will see something to lighten this long horrid winter!"

"Yes, Tituba! Read my hand!" Betty coaxed. Sitting straighter on the settle, she thrust out her small palm toward Tituba. Resignedly, the woman took it gently in her own and began tracing its lines with her brown finger.

"Such a little hand," she said softly. "Too small to hold much things. I see one tall man, handsome in his face. He come a-riding up to this door and ask for little Betty Parris to be his wife."

Betty gazed down at her hand with interest. "Do you truly see that, Tituba? And is he very handsome?"

"Oh, very!" Tituba said solemnly.

"Oh, Betty," Abigail sighed. "You are such a baby! What do you care about handsome men? Tell *my* hand, Tituba, and tell me something *real*!" She held out her hand. "Tell me, Tituba!"

"You think Tituba have nothing more to do than play games with little girls," the woman murmured, taking Abby's hand. She stared at Abigail's palm, smoothing the fingers with her own, and I saw her dark eyes widen. Then she curled the fingers inward, forming a small closed fist. "Tituba see nothing," she said, and started to rise.

"If you can see things in Betty's hand, then you can see

15

them in mine," Abby insisted. "Now, tell me! You *must* tell me!"

"Tituba don't *must* do anything, Abigail. You be but children. You best forget these nonsense things."

"There has to be something in my hand, and I want to know what it is! Do please tell me, Tituba—here!" Again Abby held out her open hand.

Taking it reluctantly, Tituba rocked gently back and forth on her stool, her eyes intent. When she spoke her voice was low, and we had to strain to hear the words.

"I see trouble," she said. "I see big trouble, and there is you, Abigail, a-kicking up your heels, right in the middle of it."

Abigail wriggled forward on the settle, her narrow eyes shining. "What kind of trouble, Tituba?"

"I told you. Big trouble. Big black trouble."

"But what *kind*?"

"A bad kind."

"And why am I kicking up my heels?"

"Child, I only tells you what I see. I no can tell you *why*."

Removing her hand from Tituba's, Abby looked at it closely. "I don't see anything," she said. "I warrant you make it all up."

"Then don't ask me what I see," Tituba said calmly. Rising from the stool, she went to the wide, scrubbed wooden table in the center of the keeping room, picked up a knife, and started scraping carrots.

"Did you really see trouble in my hand?" Abby asked.

Tituba did not answer, and the girl went on. "That would be exciting, and if you saw me kicking up my heels then I must like it—whatever it is, must I not?" Still Tituba said nothing. "Oh, Mary, would you not like Tituba to read your palm, too?"

I should very much have liked to hear what Tituba might see in my hand, but when I looked at the woman she seemed to have no interest in me. She cut the scraped carrot neatly into thirds and dropped it into an iron pot.

"Some other day, Abby, when Tituba is less busy, perhaps."

"Tituba can tell fortunes with cards, too, Mary. She can do all sorts of magic when she wants to, can't you, Tituba?"

The knife sliced into another carrot. "That for me to know," Tituba said. "Little girls like you have no need to know such things."

Abby's eyes were bright. "Tituba can put herself into a trance, Mary," she said. "Betty can do it, too, but I can't. But Tituba will teach me, won't you, Tituba?"

"No," said Tituba flatly.

"But if Betty can do it—"

"My baby be a peaceful child. If she trance herself it just be a deeper peace. But you—you is a different kind altogether!"

"What kind am I, Tituba? Tell me!"

"Don't bother me now. There be work to do. Can't trance myself out of work!"

Tituba seemed to have withdrawn from us. I hesitated,

but then asked my question anyway. "Where did you learn to—to trance yourself, Tituba?"

Another carrot was sliced into the pot before she spoke. "In Barbados," she said then. "That where I learned many things."

"What sort of things?"

"Things white people don't know."

Betty leaned forward, her hands clasped together. "Tell us," she pleaded.

Tituba let the knife cease its work and stood straight, looking over our heads into some far distant place.

"I learn things that make life be better," she said softly. "Make you warm if you is cold. Make you feel you is somewhere else if you don't fancy the place you is in. Make you feel strong inside of you, even when you is weak. In Barbados all my people know such things. Some know more than others. My grandmam taught me much. . . ."

She stood quietly for a moment, and then with a quick sigh sliced the last carrot into the heavy pot. Lifting it, she moved to the fireplace and hung it on one of the iron hooks. With her back to us she stood gazing into the flames before she spoke again. "But we not in Barbados now. Things here be very different. This Salem Village no understand how it is where John and I come from. Best you girls no think about such things. Nor you, my baby, Betty. Best you don't."

"But we *do* think about them," Abigail said with quiet satisfaction, "and you know we do, Tituba. Sometime you will teach us more of the—the 'things' you know! Some-time you will."

There came a tapping sound from the floor above and Tituba turned quickly away from the fire and started to the door that led to the hallway of the house and the steep stairs that went up from it.

"There be the mistress, a-tapping with her stick to call me," she said as she left us.

We could hear her quick steps as she mounted the stairs. I leaned toward the two younger girls.

"Can Tituba in truth do magic?" I asked.

"Of course," said Betty calmly.

"But how do you know? What have you seen her do?"

"I have seen her trance herself. And now I can do it, too."

"But I don't know what you mean," I said. "What is it, to trance yourself? What happens?"

"I don't know exactly, Mary," Betty said vaguely. "I just —oh, sometimes I sit and stare at the fire, or sometimes I stare into water—you know how quiet water is? In a bowl, or in some little pond? I look at it for a long time and then I—I go away, inside myself. It is beautiful, where I go, a place all filled with light. Heaven, it might be. It is—it is . . . well, then, it is *not* as it is here! Not cold! Just—beautiful!"

Abigail gave a little flounce of impatience. "Beautiful!" she repeated. "So it may be, but you do appear a ninny when you sit with your eyes fair pinned to the fire, taking no notice of anyone around you!"

"Then why do you want Tituba to teach you how to do it?" Betty asked.

"Oh, stuff!" Abigail got up quickly from the settle and moved restlessly about the keeping room, her long skirt over her woolen petticoats twitching as she walked. "Every day is like the day before! The same chores, the same food, the same people! If I could trance myself I would go to someplace exciting! Not just beautiful, like where Betty says she goes, but someplace where things would happen to me!"

Betty's brow wrinkled. "What sort of things, Abby? What do you wish would happen to you?"

Abby picked up a sliver of carrot from the table and crunched it between her white little teeth.

"Oh, who can say, Betty? But you know how sometimes in church meeting Uncle Samuel talks about the Devil and his works and how he lures people to do his bidding? And about the flames in Hell? And all the torments of the damned? That is what I like to listen to! *That* is exciting!"

Betty gasped. "Oh, Abby! Father just tells us such things to warn us. He does not want us to sin, for then we could not go to Heaven!"

Abigail lifted the paring knife from the table and flipped it so that it landed point down in the wood, the handle quivering.

"I think Heaven must be just like Salem Village," she said. "Everyone so good, and so pure. I become very weary of all the *Thou shalts* and *Thou shalt nots*! Someday I am going to do something shocking!"

I was amused. "What shocking thing will you do, Abby?"

"Oh, like—like—like screaming right out loud in Sabbath meeting! Just as loud as I can!"

I laughed, but poor little Betty looked distressed. "Abby! You wouldn't!"

Abigail's chin rose stubbornly. "Be not too sure, Betty Parris. For I feel at times that unless I do *something* shocking, I may blow like the cider jug and splash the whole village!"

Looking at her glittering eyes and her flushed face, I felt a certain sympathy for her. There were many times when I, too, secretly rebelled against the rigid behavior imposed on us.

I tried to sound more grown-up than I felt. "'Twill be better when you are older, Abby," I said. "I recall when I was your age, feeling that I would burst could I not shout, or run, or let my hair fly loose in the wind—but 'twill be easier soon. You will grow out of it."

Abigail eyed me closely, doubt written clear on her face. "Have *you*?" she asked.

I could not meet her gaze. I rose from my seat and moved to where my cloak and shawls hung. With my back to her I spoke calmly.

"Of course," I said. And knew I lied.

# TWO

'TWAS NOT EASY to be bound out, to be little more than a servant to people who were not your own. John Proctor was tall and straight and ruggedly handsome. He owned a tavern on the Ipswich Road, hiring others to run it for him, since he preferred to spend as much time as possible at the farm called Groton, with its seven hundred demanding acres of fertile land. Elizabeth Proctor lived here with the five children (and now a new baby was on the way), and here I, too, spent most of my time, helping in the tavern only on rare occasions.

Writing now of what took place in that bewitched time, I must leave nothing out. I must confess what I would not have admitted then to a living soul. My love! My love for John. Always to myself I called him "John," though aloud I was ever careful to say "Master Proctor." It was a love made of dreams. Dreams of his touch, dreams of his knowing someday what I felt for him, dreams of speaking openly—but none of that was possible. Instead I did all that I could to please him. No stint at the spinning wheel was too long, no amount of scrubbing and cleaning was too tiring, no amount of hours spent by the hot fire, cooking dishes I thought he might savor, was regretted if he gave some small sign of satisfaction with my work. And sometimes he did, though he was never one to praise.

Elizabeth Proctor was a kind enough mistress, though her pregnancies were hard on her, causing her to be fussy and complaining till at times I wanted to slap her. And that, of course, was a childish desire that showed I was not as mature as I had wanted Abby to believe, or even to believe myself.

As I hurried home that January afternoon I thought of Tituba and the things she claimed she knew. I wished I had asked her to tell my fortune from my hand. Could it ever include John? The very possibility made me shiver and I swore I would have my palm read the next time I was with Tituba. John and me! Elizabeth gone somewhere, anywhere —I truly did not anticipate *how* she would be gone. Just John and me together! To be close to him, to touch him— even the thought made me weak. I quickened my steps to reach home the sooner, and at a turn in the road nigh knocked over old Goody Good and little Dorcas, her daughter.

The old woman, who could not, I know, have been near as old as she seemed, peered at me through folds of filthy shawls and wisps of straggling hair, her reeking pipe clenched between her few remaining yellowed teeth.

"In a great hurry, ain't we, girl!" Her voice grated on me with its high pitch. "Cannot wait to get back to your handsome master, eh?"

I tried to be calm. "'Tis frigid cold, Mistress Good. I have no desire to linger on the way."

"Very wise. John Proctor is not above taking the whipping stick to his jade, do he think it needed."

The idea made the blood rush to my face, and I knew the old crone saw it.

"Master Proctor does not believe in whipping," I said, trying to keep my voice steady.

"The more fool he, then. Dorcas and I will stop by later, I fancy. If *Master* Proctor is so kind he might find some scraps of food for us. The belly itself gets cold with nothing to warm it."

Though it would have been only Christian to feel sorry for her, I could not. I knew her husband was a lazy man who worked a bit from time to time if anyone would hire him, spending the few pence he made on drink, so that Goody Good was forced to beg for whatever she would have. Yet, even knowing this, I still wanted to back away from her, away from the stench of unwashed flesh and garments and hair, away from the horrible smell of her pipe. Heaven knew what she had been smoking in it! The child, Dorcas, no more than four years old, clutched her mother's skirt with a dirty, reddened hand, and stared at me with dark solemn eyes. Shifting as if to leave them, I pulled my cloak closer about me.

"I am sure Master Proctor will find something for you," I said, and hurried away.

Behind me I heard the old woman's cackling laugh.

"Think you know him pretty well, don't 'e? He's a hard man, is John Proctor, but we'll see. We'll see."

"Old witch," I muttered to myself, and made my way back to Groton as swiftly as I could.

During the next day or so I thought often of the strange conversation that had taken place at the Parris house. Searching for an excuse to return, I bethought me of a piece of needlework I had started.

"'Tis a new stitch Abby Williams showed me," I told Mistress Proctor, "but I must not have watched her carefully. If I might ask her again—"

She gave permission, and I left the house as quickly as I could, heading straight for the Parris keeping room. I can still see that room so clearly. It was not unlike many others in the houses of Salem Village. They were all warm, and sometimes in the summer overly so, since the cooking fires still needed to burn bright. They all had wood piled to feed the hungry blaze; pails of water, carefully covered to keep insects from falling into them; scoured tables and long comfortable settles and small stools. All had fragrant bunches of herbs hanging from the raftered ceilings, drying, waiting to be dropped by the sprig into a boiling soup kettle, or pounded into powder and stored in heavy crocks to be used later in food or as medications. Perhaps one difference lay in the herbs themselves, for there were unfamiliar ones in the Parris kitchen that Tituba claimed to have brought with her from that far, mysterious Barbados.

Though they looked as dry and gray-brown as all the others, they seemed to send a more exotic scent into the room, as strange and exciting as the island they came from.

I smelled them now as I opened the door, then instantly forgot them in astonishment at the number of people in the room. Betty Parris, Abby Williams, and Tituba, of course. But there was Mary Walcott with her knitting, which she scarce needed to watch, so skillful were her fingers. Mary was seventeen, and lived with her aunt, Mistress Mary Sibley. Elizabeth Booth and Susanna Sheldon sat near the fire. Elizabeth was sixteen then, and Susanna two years older, and both were bound girls as I was. I saw twelve-year-old Anne Putnum, a thin, tense child with enormous pale eyes, and Mercy Lewis, a rosy, happy girl who was bound to the Putnums.

Tituba was the center of attention. She sat, back erect, her white-turbaned head bent over cards she had laid out upon the table. The room was deep in silence, as if every girl were holding her breath, awaiting Tituba's words. When a burning stick in the great fireplace snapped, I jumped.

Tituba looked intently at the cards spread before her, muttering something I could not catch. Then she gathered them together, working them in her hands, and laid them out again.

"What is it, Tituba?" Anne Putnum asked. "Tell us what the cards say."

"I have no liking for what the cards say," Tituba murmured, and again she gathered and reworked them.

Abby Williams sighed impatiently. "You sit there and stare at the cards, so they must say something. I want to know what it is!"

"You is a child wants to know too much. There be trouble in the cards, and Tituba goes better with no trouble."

"What kind of trouble?"

"Abigail, I told you—that day I looked at your hand—I told you there was big black trouble waiting! I try the cards, I think they may say different, but they tell the same thing. Now leave me be!"

"I don't like trouble," little Betty Parris whimpered, and her large eyes brimmed with tears. "Do not ask any more, Abby, please!"

Abigail folded her arms over her flat chest, sitting very straight. "Tituba told us she would read the cards for us," she said, "and she must! I want to know what they say! It may be that Tituba just says whatever she chooses, and there is naught in the silly cards at all!"

Tituba turned her dark, glowing eyes on Abby, and her face was stern. "You say that 'cause you affrighted to hear. If you did not believe in Tituba you would not pesk her to tell you things!"

"I am not afraid of anything, and you said you would tell us. *Saying* you see trouble doesn't mean 'tis *so*! Now, tell!"

Tituba gazed at Abigail for a long moment, her face unreadable. Then she lowered her eyes to the cards that lay spread on the table.

"Very well, then," she said. "I tell you. There is trouble

such as you have never seen. Worse trouble than you little girls can think of."

"We have seen the smallpox," Anne Putnum said. "Surely no trouble can be worse than that."

"This be worse."

"As bad as the fire that destroyed two houses last month?" That was Mary Walcott, her fingers moving rapidly with needles and wool.

"This be far worse, for this be hellfire."

Huddled in a corner of the settle, Betty Parris covered her eyes with her hands and sobbed. Abigail glanced at her with impatience.

"Stop that, Betty," she said sharply. "'Tis all in sport! Be not so babyish!" Abigail turned back to Tituba. "How can the cards tell of something worse than the smallpox? Or fire?" she demanded.

"God send the sickness and the flames," Tituba replied. "But this—what I see in the cards—this come not from God."

"From where, then?"

"This trouble come from you, Abigail Williams! From you, from each one of you! You is all here, all you girls, and you hear me now! You is going to make people suffer worse than God do!"

Susanna Sheldon, blue eyes wide in her plain face, clasped her hands tight together in her lap. "But we—why should we make people suffer, Tituba? We are but ordinary girls. We do no harm."

"The harm be coming! And it come from all of you! There be blackness in some and it will pass to the others." She stabbed a forefinger at the cards. "It be all here. Trouble—blackness—the Devil himself—and death!"

It was then that Betty Parris shrieked and started to scream, so that we all but fell from our seats. She sat stiffly, as if frozen, her eyes tight shut, her face contorted, her fists clenched, scream after scream coming from her mouth. With a quick movement Tituba dashed the cards to the floor and went to Betty.

"Betty baby! Hush now! It be all nonsense, what the cards say. My baby must not fret herself!" Tituba tried to take Betty into her arms, but the child pulled away, her screams continuing as if she were powerless to stop them.

Mercy Lewis clapped her hands over her ears, her round face crumpling into tears. "Make her stop," she begged. "Make Betty stop that!"

Abigail's narrow eyes shone. "She's having a fit," she announced with relish. "That's what it is—a fit!"

At that moment Betty's father burst through the keeping-room door. He must have been in the small room he used as a study, working on one of his sermons, for his sandy hair was ruffled as if he had been running his fingers through it, and he grasped a Bible in one hand and a quill pen in the other.

"What is going on?" he demanded. "How can a man set down the words of the Gospel in such a furor? If you girls cannot be quiet—" His eyes went to Betty, as well they might, considering the screams that still rang through the room. "Betty! What childish nonsense is this? I am trying to listen to the voice of God and all I can hear is—"

As he father said "God," Betty's eyes flew open. She gave one last shriek, threw her arms about Tituba, and sobbed quietly. Reverend Parris drew a deep sigh of relief.

"There, that is better," he said, "though you know that I do not approve of babyish weeping, daughter. Dry your eyes now, and let me get on with my work." He moved to the door, saying, "Ah, it is not easy to be a man of God!" His last word seemed to echo as the door closed after him, and Betty shuddered violently, held close in Tituba's warm arms.

For a moment there was silence. Then Abigail grasped Betty's shoulder and shook it, demanding her attention. "Betty! What took you? It was a fit, wasn't it?"

Betty lifted her head from Tituba's bosom and looked round the room at our stunned faces. Her expression was perfectly calm, her eyes wide and luminous. "Whatever are you all gaping at?" she asked. "Is something wrong with you?"

We looked at each other in wonder. "With *us*?" Anne Putnum asked. "'Twas you, Betty, screeching like the hounds of Hell were upon you!"

"Nonsense," Betty said primly. "You are imagining things." And sitting back on the settle, she straightened her cap, smoothed her dress, and smiled on us all. "Now," she said, "tell us what the cards truly say, Tituba."

With a long look at the little girl, Tituba rose, picked the strewn cards from the floor, and gathered them into a neat stack.

"No," she said. "Tituba has work to do."

# THREE

MORE SNOW FELL that night, and before John Proctor left in the morning for one of his rare visits to his tavern he paused beside me as I was sweeping the kitchen hearth.

"The new snow is not deep," he said. "I have left the shovel by the door. Clear the path, Mary, lest it freeze and become treacherous for your mistress. In her condition a fall could be dangerous."

"Yes, sir," I breathed, gazing up at his rough hair and deep-set blue eyes.

"You were very silent last night. Is aught wrong with you? You are in good health?"

"Oh, yes, sir! 'Twas just—oh, 'twas nothing."

"You had best tell me."

"Oh, little Betty Parris had a screaming fit yesterday. I cannot put it out of my mind."

He smiled, making pleasant crinkles beside his eyes. "Judging from my own, I would say children scream a great deal. That should not surprise you."

I looked down. There was no way I could explain to him how strangely frightening it had been. "No, sir," I said.

"You will not forget about the path."

"No, sir," I said again, and he left. The room seemed empty without him.

So it was that an hour or so later I was shoveling the path that led from the kitchen door when Abigail Williams came by, wrapped warm against the cold, her eyes sparkling in her thin face.

"How is Betty?" I asked. "Is she recovered today?"

"I suppose some might say so, but she is not! Oh, Mary, if you had but been with us last night when Uncle Samuel held our evening prayers!"

"'Tis bad enough here when Master Proctor holds ours," I said. "The heat from the fire makes me sleepy, and though the prayers are not of great length, still my knees do tire—"

"Oh, stuff!" Abby interrupted, twitching her red cloak tighter about her. "*We* must have prayers in Uncle's study where there is no fire, and the floor is so hard my bones creak, and he goes on and on and on—but last night, oh, Mary! You will never believe!" Those sly blue eyes were filled with excitement.

"How can I believe what I don't know?" I asked, and slid the shovel under the snow, filling it and throwing the snow aside. "You are telling me nothing!"

"Hush, and I will tell you! And stop shoveling! You must listen! So, last night at prayers, Uncle Samuel finished his reading from the Bible, and began the praying, which he seems dearly to love for he has much to say to God, and he asked God to give his daughter control over 'unseemly displays of emotion'—that is how he put it, Mary. And all of

33

a sudden Betty fell flat forward on the floor and started screeching again until I thought my ears would burst, and she kicked her feet till she split the toe of her shoe, and she beat her hands on the floor, and shrieked and shrieked. And then I felt I was going to do the same thing—I could feel the screams coming up in my throat just from listening to her, and I wanted to leap around the room and make a great noise, and it was all so strange and exciting, and the next thing I knew I was running round and round and flapping my arms and shouting and it was the most wonderful feeling!" She paused, gasping for breath in the cold air.

All I could say was, "Abigail! You could not have!"

"But I did! And the oddest thing was that I hardly knew what I was doing! Tituba picked Betty up—Aunt Elizabeth had not come down to prayers because she felt the room was too cold and her coughing would start again—and John Indian just knelt there, staring, and then Uncle Samuel shouted at me, 'Abigail! Have you gone mad?' And I didn't really hear him, not really, and then he caught me and gave my face a slap, and I looked around and I didn't know quite what had been happening, and I felt so *wonderful*! It was almost as good as standing up in church and screaming, and I have always wanted to do that! You know I have!"

"But, Abigail!" I was nigh speechless. "How *could* you have behaved so?"

Her laugh was high-pitched and breathless. "I do not know. I saw Betty, and heard her, and then the strongest feeling came over me. I just had to—to—let go of myself! 'Twas very strange, indeed!"

"What did Reverend Parris do then?"

"He sent us to bed, Betty and me, and went up to talk to Aunt Elizabeth. And this morning at breakfast he looked as if we might fly up to the rafters right before his eyes!" She laughed again. "Poor Uncle Samuel! We did give him a fright!"

"I should think so, indeed!"

"Don't look so put out, Mary! I can't tell you how—how *exciting* it was! Like, oh, like being drenched with a cool rain after a stifling summer's day!"

I stared at her, and could feel the disapproval on my face. "I think I prefer a drink of cool water to being drenched by it," I said, and slid the shovel under the snow again.

She gave another quick little laugh. "Dear cautious Mary!" she said. "But come to our house this afternoon, for I mean to make Tituba tell us what the cards say. Nothing could be as terrible as she seems to believe, and I must know what she sees! Will you come?"

"I do not know," I said. "Perhaps."

"You will," Abby said confidently, and skipped back to the road.


And of course I did. Elizabeth Proctor was not mean about allowing a fair amount of freedom, and she did not object when I asked if I might go for a walk. Why did I not want to tell her where the walk would take me? Even then I must have sensed that it was wrong, but I felt pulled there by some force I could not resist.

The sky was a clear blue, the sun was shining, but with little warmth, and the snow was blindingly white and clean. I went quickly along the road to the crossing where I had met Goody Good, and then along the side road to the Parris house. I was almost there when I saw, coming from the opposite direction, Elizabeth Hubbard and Sarah Churchill. Sarah was bound out to George Jacobs, a sharp-tongued old man, toothless and lame, who could get about only with the aid of two canes. Elizabeth was an orphan (as the smallpox had made so many of us) and lived with her aunt, Mistress Griggs, wife of the doctor. As we met I greeted them and asked where they were going. They looked at each other almost guiltily before they replied, and then it was Sarah who spoke.

"We thought to visit the Parris house," she said. "We have heard of strange goings-on that take place there. Do you know aught of it?"

"Little," I told her, "though I have been there and seen Betty Parris in some sort of a taking, and Abigail Williams has told me the same happened again last night at prayers."

"But what of the slave, Tituba?" Elizabeth asked. "'Tis said she can read one's hand, or the cards, and see the future. That is what we want to hear!"

"She has said but little when I have been there, and all of it filled with mystery and doom."

"What doom can hang over us?" Elizabeth asked lightly.

"And surely there is no mystery about us! In any case, are you going there, too?" Almost ashamed, I nodded. "Then come! We must not miss any of the circus!"

And so it was that we three arrived together to find the keeping room nigh filled with girls. All who had been there yesterday were there again, and now with Elizabeth Hubbard and Sarah and me there were ten of us, all clustered around Tituba, who sat like a queen at the table. On it were her cards, tarot cards she called them, and a shallow bowl of water.

That day she told our fortunes, though what she made up and what she may have "seen" I could not say, for her soft voice hesitated many times as if she chose not to speak of all that the cards showed her. She told Betty she would go on a long visit, but she could not, or would not, say where. She told Anne Putnum that her strength would become her undoing, which made little sense to any of us, and she told Mercy Lewis of a sickness that would all but kill her. She told Elizabeth Hubbard that she would look with her uncle, Dr. Griggs, upon such illness as had not been known before. I do not recall what other predictions Tituba made.

When at last it was my turn she stared at the cards for some moments before she spoke.

"A tall man," she said, "not young. He be close to you." I felt a shiver of excitement. The tall man, not young, was surely John. "But there be something 'tween you," Tituba went on. "Something—"

"What?" I whispered. "What is between us?"

"A darkness. A great wall of darkness." Her eyes lifted from the cards and looked straight into mine. "Give me your hand," she said.

I held it out and could feel myself trembling as she delicately traced the lines in my palm.

"That man," Tituba said. "You hold his life in this hand, girl. That is all I have to tell you."

My mind whirled, thinking of ways in which I might rescue John from some danger, save him from some unknown fate. Tituba saw darkness between us, but I would cross that darkness to help him, for I held his life in my hands! I felt giddy with happiness at the thought.

Suddenly Anne Putnum spoke softly. "Look at Betty."

Betty sat stiffly, staring with unblinking eyes at the bowl of water on the table.

"She has tranced herself again," Abigail said, and the pleasure in her voice was evident. She leaned toward her cousin. "Betty," she whispered. "Betty Parris." The little girl did not move nor appear to hear. Abby clapped her hands sharply together, shouting Betty's name, and slowly Betty turned her head.

"You made me come back," she said reproachfully. "Why did you do that?"

"Oh, stuff! You were not anywhere but here. How could you come back?"

"I was not here. I was flying over a wide blue lake, and over trees, and into sunshine. I was not here."

Tense, pale-eyed little Anne Putnum began to shake.

"That is what witches do," she said. "'Tis said that the body of a witch may be in one place while the witch herself is flying high above!"

"My baby's no witch," Tituba said firmly. "You is not to say such things."

"I did not say Betty was a witch," Anne said bravely. "I said that witches can do that. And we all know there *are* witches—the Bible tells us so. The Devil cannot do all his work alone, he must have others to aid him—and who better than a child who looks young and innocent, and can do her work unsuspected? Surely that might be the Devil's choice."

Mercy Lewis, the girl who lived and worked in Anne's house, spoke quickly. "Do not say such things, Anne Putnum! Betty is no more a witch than I am!"

"And who is to know that you are not?" Anne's thin voice was sharp. "And Tituba! Surely you are a witch, Tituba—tell us!"

Calmly the dark-skinned woman gazed at Anne. "There be many witches in Barbados," she said thoughtfully, "but they be not like witches here in this cold white place. In Barbados there be good witches who can cure bad sickness, and bring love to those who want it. They have potions and ways to do these things."

"And do you have these potions—and *ways*, Tituba?" Anne persisted.

Instead of answering directly, Tituba carefully moved the bowl of water closer to Anne. "Look into that bowl of water, Anne Putnum," she said, "and tell me what you see."

"I see nothing!"

"Because you no look. Look deep into it, now, keep your eyes wide, look, look deep. Say what you see."

With a strange reluctance Anne turned her eyes to the bowl of water, gazing into it while Tituba spoke softly. None of us dared breathe.

"Look deep, child, deep into the water. There are deep things in the water—things to see, things to know." Over and over Tituba repeated such words. At last she said, "Now. Tell me what you see."

Time seemed to stop before Anne spoke. When at last she did, her voice sounded as if it came from a long distance. It was faint, so faint we could barely hear her, and infinitely sad.

"I see the babies—my mother's babies—all those who were born before me and died so young. They lie there . . . white in their winding sheets . . . their hands are stretched out to me. They are crying. I cannot help them." Her voice rose. "I cannot *help* them!"

With a terrible cry Anne covered her face with her hands and wept, small screams coming with tears. A moment more and Betty joined her.

"I see them, too," she moaned. "They have no faces! They frighten me!" And throwing her head back so that it cracked against the settle, she shrieked.

In a trice the room was like Bedlam! One after another,

the girls screamed and moaned and beat their heads with their hands. Only Mary Walcott and I sat silent, Mary going on with her knitting while her wide eyes went from face to face, I with a cold, sick fear flowing through me as I fought against joining my shrieks with the others.

# FOUR

FOR THREE DAYS I held myself away from the Parris house. It seemed to me three weeks. I scrubbed clothes, I washed and polished windows, I swept the floors, I cut kindling for the fires, I scoured pots and kettles, trying to exhaust the pounding energy I felt. My whole body longed for some sort of release. If I could have screamed as the girls screamed, or drummed my feet against the floor as Betty had, or beaten my head with my hands! My body seemed to hold a small fire that needed to burst into flame before it could burn itself out and give me peace. And each day was worse than the one before, so that on the fourth day I fled and joined the others in Reverend Parris's keeping room.

They were all there, and the very sight of the other girls eased me. Most of them were working dutifully on some piece of sewing or knitting, talking idly and calmly together. What had I been afraid of? We were young innocent girls. These were my friends. I could not think what had caused my deep unrest through the past three days!

"You are back with us, Mary," Elizabeth Hubbard said. "We have missed you."

"I was behind in my chores. I had much to do."

"It is best when we are all together," Abigail said. "We were just speaking of the strange goings-on when Tituba told Anne to gaze into the bowl of water. Do you recall?" I nodded. "I doubt that Anne truly saw anything in that bowl," Abby went on. "What could she have seen? 'Twas just water."

Anne Putnum looked up from the small stitches she was taking in the hem of an apron. Her thin face seemed even smaller, closely framed by her cap, and her lips were pressed tight together.

"I saw just what I told of. I thought, like you, that I should see naught, but they were there, in that water, all those dead babies my mother bore and buried. Plainly I saw them, their arms reached out . . ." Suddenly she shivered and dropped her eyes to her hemming.

"I do not believe you," Abigail said flatly.

"I care not what you believe, Abigail Williams. I know well what I saw!"

"Mistress Putnum speaks often of those infants," Mercy Lewis said in her slow, quiet voice. "I have heard her many times. Sometimes she weeps when she thinks of them."

"True," admitted Abigail. "I, too, have heard her. I expect that was in your mind, Anne, and you simply spoke of it."

"'Twas not in my mind! I did not believe Tituba had all the powers she said she had. I did not believe she could truly see our futures in the cards nor in our hands. And then she told me to look in the water—and I *saw*! I saw those babies! It was horrible!" Dropping her sewing, Anne put her hands over her eyes.

Abby gazed thoughtfully at her, the long narrow eyes secretive. "If Anne could see such clear pictures in a bowl of water, what might not the rest of us see if we tried?"

"I saw the babies, too," Betty Parris reminded them, her small voice high and clear. "'Twasn't just Anne."

"True, Betty. And surely, if two of us saw strange things in the water, others might do the same." Abby's voice was too quiet, too calm. It made me strangely uneasy.

"I think 'tis best forgotten," I said. "Neither Anne nor Betty liked what they saw."

"I was frightened!" Betty said. "So frightened I screamed!"

"So you must have believed in what you saw," Abby murmured. Then she looked up at us and smiled. "Tituba is not here to help us. Aunt Elizabeth has sent her on an errand. But perhaps we can see things by ourselves. How interesting that would be!" The blue eyes, beginning to sparkle now, slid from face to face. "I shall try first!"

Anne Putnum lifted her head. "And you will see nothing and will say I am a liar!"

"But Betty saw what you did, Anne. Surely I would not call my own cousin a liar. Oh, come! Let us have a little amusement!"

I did not know what was in Abby's mind, but I did not trust her. Those sly eyes . . . "Do you think we should?" I asked.

"Oh, Mary, be not so prim! What harm can it do? And I am weary of sewing!"

She rose quickly, dropping her needlework on the settle behind her. Her face was suddenly flushed with excitement.

"Do you want the bowl of water, Abby?" Mary Walcott asked, her fingers knitting rapidly as if with a life of their own.

"No, I shall try without the water. I shall just close my eyes and think! But you must all help me!"

"But what are we to do?" Mercy asked. "We know nothing of these things."

Abigail gave a short gasp of laughter. "Then let us learn!" she said. She took a stand before the great fireplace, her back to the flames, her arms straight at her sides, her head lifted, her eyes tight closed.

For a moment she stood silent and unmoving. When she spoke her voice was hushed, barely a whisper.

"I am looking into darkness," she began. "I am looking into deep black darkness. My eyes are shut against the world. I am clearing my mind of all things. I am alone, standing in darkness. I feel the heat of the fire on my back."

Uncontrollably Sarah Churchill giggled. Betty Parris, leaning forward, her eyes intent on her cousin, muttered, "Hush!"

Abigail's high voice deepened. "In the darkness I can see whirls of color, brilliant, like the sun glittering on the sea. It blinds me!" She squeezed her eyes tighter. "Now the

*45*

darkness rushes in again . . . there is no light. . . I am all alone in the dark—wait! The dark becomes red, red mixed with blackness. A shape is forming . . . a figure. I cannot see it well. It is tall . . . it is taller than I. It stands above me—" Abby's head lifted, her eyes still clenched shut.

No one was laughing now. I felt a grip on my wrist, and, looking down, saw Anne Putnum's hand holding my arm in a grasp that whitened her knuckles.

"I cannot see the figure clearly," Abby's voice went on. "It is tall . . . and dark. It looms over me. It is black now, against the red. It is close to me—" The girl took a step back. "I see its long legs. It is coming closer . . . closer . . . closer . . . " She began moving slowly, edging round in a circle, her hands raised in front of her. Beside me Anne moaned softly. "I see no face . . . just great white teeth, like a dog's fangs. There are hands with long, hairy fingers. It comes closer . . . closer—" Suddenly her scream ripped through the room and my ears rang with it. "'Tis the Devil!" she shrieked. "'Tis Satan! His hands—his hands— his hands—"

Falling to the floor in a small heap, Abigail wrapped her arms about her head, swaying from side to side, still screaming. I could stand it no longer. In a flash I rose and bent over her, pulling her arms free and lifting her face. Her eyes were still tight shut, and I drew back my hand and slapped her blind face. The screaming stopped on a high note. Then Abigail's eyes opened slowly and she stared at me as if she had never seen me before. In all the room there was no sound. Abigail, eleven-year-old Abigail, gazed up at me.

"I saw the Devil," she said, and her words came slowly. "He is vastly tall, and black, and his hands reached out for me."

Without a sound Betty Parris slipped from the settle onto the floor in a dead faint. Abigail looked at her, and slowly a smile came over her face. She stood up, smoothing down her tumbled skirts.

"You see?" she said calmly. "We can do such things ourselves. Look at Betty. She knows. We have no need of Tituba, nor of bowls of water. We are enough. Now, which of you would choose to be next?"

But no one chose. We ministered to Betty, bathing her face, speaking softly to her, until she opened her eyes.

"I saw him, too," she whispered. "I saw the Devil, too."

Almost silently we gathered our shawls and our handwork together, and with not more than a word or two we left. The fresh cold air out of doors seemed like the very breath of life.

# FIVE

EVEN THEN we could have stopped. Back in the busy, homely atmosphere of the Proctors' house I swore I would have no more to do with the girls when they indulged in their newfound sport. I told myself it was naught but nonsense and silly imaginings, and then I would think of Abby's face when I slapped her. She had said, "I saw the Devil." And I remembered the soft weight of little Betty's unconscious body, and I could hear her whisper, "I saw the Devil, too." And I knew that whatever it was, it was no longer nonsense, and that I had to know whatever more there was to know. There had been a nameless power in that room and I had seen it . . . felt it.

And the days went on and we met in the warm keeping room, and sometimes Tituba was there with her cards and her prophecies, and sometimes we, some of us, managed to put ourselves into that strange state where we knew naught of the room around us but filled our eyes with dark and unknown creatures, and sometimes we cried out in fear at what we saw. And yet we would not stop. The power was within ourselves, and stayed with us even when we were not together.

As hard as he might try, it was impossible for Reverend Parris to stay in ignorance of what was happening in his kitchen on those winter afternoons. Sanity seemed to have deserted his household, and even though he was closed in with his pen, his Bible, and his thoughts, he could not help but hear the screams and wails and sobs that came from his keeping room. As for Betty's mother, that poor woman, beset by the noise, pulled herself from her bed, wrapped herself in shawls, and came with cold bare feet to see what went on. Mistress Parris staggered into the room, collapsing on a settle in such a spasm of coughing that she could not speak. Clutching her chest against the pain, she tried to gasp out questions, but a hush settled over all of us and she learned nothing.

That evening, however, she came downstairs again, moving slowly, to join in the family prayers. Thus it was that she was there to see Betty, head high when all others were reverently bowed, staring straight ahead into space, fists tight, lips drawn back from her teeth. Whenever Samuel Parris mentioned the name of the Almighty, Betty made a sound nigh to a beast's growl. When the Reverend began his prayer, exhorting God to look upon these stricken children, she screamed aloud, thudding the floor with her feet, pulling at her hair. Instantly Abby crouched on all fours and went racing about the room, barking and snarling like a dog. The prayer session came to an abrupt end, Mistress Parris was taken in a swoon to her bed by an expressionless John Indian, and Reverend Parris resorted again to prayer, this time by himself.

In the Sibley house that same evening Mary Walcott sat talking to Susanna Sheldon of what they had seen in the Parris kitchen, when suddenly Susanna went into convulsions and within seconds Mary, too, was afflicted.

When news of this spread, as it inevitably and rapidly did, the same misfortune descended on the house of Thomas Putnum, where Anne Putnum and Mercy Lewis writhed on the floor, screaming as their muscles knotted painfully. Anne's limbs became so contorted her parents had to hold her firmly, lest she break the bones.

Now panic came to all of Salem Village. What caused these takings? Who would be next? For in a few days it developed that each of the ten girls who frequented the Parris home had been stricken with a seizure at one time or another. And I? Oh, yes, I, too.

It happened on a dark moonless night when I lay in my narrow bed at John Proctor's farm, tossing in my search for sleep. In the winter silence I kept hearing voices. Anne's, when she gazed into the bowl of clear water. Abby's, when she said she had seen the Devil. Tituba's, when she spoke of hellfire that was coming. I heard screeching, and the thud of small feet on wooden floors, and the crack of Betty's head against the settle, and screaming again, and moaning, and weeping. My heart seemed close to exploding through my chest. My nails dug into the flesh of my hands as I clenched them, and my skin was icy, and with no will of my own I opened my mouth and shrieked. And could not stop.

The door to my room flew open and John stood there, tall in his nightshirt, his nightcap askew upon his head, a lighted candle in his hand. Striding to the side of the bed, he looked down at me.

"What the devil ails you, girl?" he roared, trying to be heard above my screams. I could not answer.

Going to the washstand, he set the candle down, picked up the pitcher of icy water, and dashed a fair amount of it in my face. The screaming stopped as I glared up at him, and then I burst into tears. Curling into as tight a ball as I could, I hid my face and wept. John replaced the pitcher and thrust a towel at me.

"Dry yourself," he ordered, "and then tell me what insanity has taken you."

How could I explain? To one who had not heard nor seen what I had, the story would seem ridiculous. I tried, but even to my own ears it sounded like infantile maunderings. John stood beside my bed, shivering in the freezing night air. I repeated myself nigh a dozen times, saying again and again, "If you had heard them—or seen them—the screams . . ." At last he spoke.

"Hysterical females," he said coldly. "Aye, I have heard some talk of these seizures about the village, but I had not thought to have one in my own house. You will not visit the Parrises again unless I give permission, Mary. Is that clear?" I nodded, trying to still the foolish sobs. "The spinning is way behind," he added. "See that you get to it tomorrow."

"Yes, sir," I whispered.

With a rough pat on my shoulder, he left the room, taking the candle with him and leaving me in darkness. My skin felt warm where his hand had touched me. The rest of my body was icy cold.

In a village as small as Salem all that went on was common knowledge, and now the main concern of the people was our circle of young girls. Villagers recalled the family of God-fearing John Goodwin of Boston, whose children had fallen victims to just such seizures four years before, and had terrified everyone with their insane babblings and crazed antics. Ministers gathered and prayed over them, to no avail. At last the finger was pointed at a washerwoman, a Goody Glover, whom many had suspected of being a witch. Witch Glover was hanged, but it was not for some time after that the four Goodwin children were restored to their senses. Everyone in Salem Village had heard of Witch Glover, and a few of them had journeyed to Boston to watch the hanging, taking their children with them since, of course, such an exhibition would be an excellent object lesson to a child. So it was not surprising that now, in Salem Village, the word *witchcraft* began to be whispered about.

Reverend Parris was not a stupid man, nor an overly superstitious one, and he refused to heed the whispers. Instead he waited until an evening when Betty and Abigail began the twitching and moaning that betokened one of their attacks, and then he and John Indian carried them bodily to the home of Dr. Griggs. Elizabeth Hubbard, Mrs. Griggs's orphaned niece, opened the door, took one look at the two twisting, babbling figures, and started to twitch and grunt and moan herself. Into this walked Dr. Griggs.

Poor man! If we did not know what afflicted us, how could he? He consulted his books, he questioned and noted. Within a few days he saw each of us except me.

"Mary needs no doctor," said John Proctor flatly, when Reverend Parris asked him to allow me to be examined. And that was all he would say. But for the rest, good Dr. Griggs went from house to house visiting his troubled patients. He tried physics of various sorts, nostrums, concoctions, brews—none of them had any effect. The girls continued to jibber and jabber, to fling themselves from one end of the room to the other, to moan and groan and weep and scream. And in each case, Dr. Griggs observed, as soon as the wild antics ceased and sanity seemed restored, the girls looked as rested and happy as if naught but the sunniest good fortune had befallen them. On one occasion the doctor, thumbing through his medical books, came upon *Epilepsy*, and was sure he had found his diagnosis, but further reading removed even that possibility. Finally, his words to Reverend Parris were, "The evil hand is on them."

And now, indeed, Salem Village fell into a dither! The favored theory was that the girls were possessed, and that, of course, meant that the Devil was afoot in the little town, searching for young souls to make his own. And since the Devil must needs have helpers to pursue his work, it followed that there must be witches. But who? And where?

Other villagers, of whom John Proctor was certainly one,

disagreed. Did no one notice, they asked, how rosy and fresh and happy the girls appeared when they came out of their takings? Did no one notice that they were now the center of all attention, just the thing to please a young girl's vanity? Did no one notice that their fits took them only when there was an interested audience? John announced that I had been cured by sitting at the spinning wheel under the threat of a sound thrashing should I move without permission (though in fact he had never raised his hand against me), and advocated such treatment for all the afflicted.

The fact of the matter was that I had been forbidden to leave the Proctor farm, and knew only as much of what went on as I could glean from John's or Mistress Proctor's scant remarks. This enforced solitude had a divided effect —on the one hand making me much calmer in my mind, with no wild voices to excite me, on the other causing me to wish urgently that I could again join that circle and allow myself the release of the noise and movement and mystery.

There were several taverns in Salem Village besides John's, and one was a most respectable and homey place known as Ingersoll's ordinary. It stood close to the Parris house, and John Indian often worked there as helper to Deacon Nathaniel Ingersoll and his wife, Sarah, who ran the place. The ordinary was very much the center of Salem Village, with all manner of people stopping in for a drop of ale or cider, or a hot meat pasty, or simply to sit by the roaring fire and gossip. There came a morning when Mistress Proctor sent me there on an errand, carrying a large sack of goose down to Sarah Ingersoll for the making of quilts. Although the sack was large, it had little weight and I walked quickly, glad to be out of doors again, and away, for a time at least, from the accursed spinning wheel.

As I opened the door to the ordinary and stepped inside I suddenly dropped the sack, for there was Abigail Williams rolling on the wide plank floor in front of the fire, thrumming her heels on the floor and screaming.

I stood there, staring at her, and my blood began to pound. The rest of the room faded from my sight until there was only the blaze of the fire and Abby. My ears filled with her screams; my breathing grew so quick that it choked me. My hands were suddenly damp, I could feel beads of sweat on my brow, my knees weakened. Slowly I fell to the floor and my scream joined Abby's as I, too, rolled and thrummed my feet against the wooden boards. It was as if there had been a tightness in me that must have release, as if bonds that pinioned me were stricken off. I knew as from a great distance what I was doing, I could not stop myself, and I cared not. I relished it! I could barely see the white shocked faces that were turned upon us.

It was not until Abigail tried to throw herself into the fire and was held by a dozen sturdy customers who soothed and petted and comforted her—not until then did I, too, seem to come to my senses, sitting up with what must have been the look of a sheep upon my face, then hastening to smooth my apparel and regain what little dignity might be left me. All about the room there was the hum of voices.

"Possessed! They are possessed! The poor children . . . not strong enough to fight the black power that takes them . . . poor Abigail . . . poor Mary—possessed!"

That was the word that was repeated, that hissing, snake-like word, *possessed*. And in truth that is what I felt—that some unnameable thing was forcing me into these fits, something I was powerless to fight, did not want to fight. It was a terrifying thought!

Kind Sarah Ingersoll came to me, murmuring soft words, helping me tidy my clothing, accepting the sack of goose down and thanking me for its delivery, trying in every gentle way she knew to comfort me. I was grateful to her, but I could not wait to leave the tavern. When I did, it was to find Abigail by my side. She was cheerful, her bright face smiling composedly from out the red hood that framed it, and she hummed softly as we walked a little way together. After a few steps I could bear it no longer.

"Abby, what is happening to us?" I asked.

"Happening? Why, really, Mary, who can say?" She gave me one of her sly, sidelong glances, her eyes gleaming, and I could have sworn that she winked at me.

"Will you be at church meeting tomorrow?" she asked.

"Of course. Why would I not? We do always attend."

"'Twas an idle question. We have not seen you in the past few days. It will be pleasant if we are all together again. All us poor possessed little girls!"

With a merry laugh she turned and walked primly toward the Parris house.

# SIX

DURING THE FEW DAYS that I had been kept at home by the Proctors, much had been taking place in Salem Village. Since Dr. Griggs had used the phrase "the evil hand is on them," no further thought was given to trying to cure us of our fits by medical means. Reverend Parris reasoned that if our bodies were not to blame, then it must be our souls, and this being within his province as minister, he set to work. He enlisted the aid of several ministers from the towns around Salem Village, such as Beverly and Ipswich and Salem Town, to add their prayers to his and to search with him for the cause of this most dreadful affliction.

When I followed Elizabeth and John Proctor into the church that Sabbath, it was to see two of these worthy men beside Reverend Parris. On his right was fierce Nicholas Noyes from Salem Town, and on his left mild John Hale from Beverly. The three solemn faces watched as the villagers entered and seated themselves. There seemed to be a current running through the meetinghouse—faint whispers, the craning of necks to see where the "poor possessed girls" were sitting, small restless movements. It was as though the congregation had gathered with the expectation of entertainment rather than of pious devotion. They had not long to wait.

Reverend Parris, his voice rising strong and clear in the crowded building, began his sermon. At the first sacred word he uttered, Abigail shrieked as if she had been bitten; at the second she was joined by two or three of the rest of us; at the third there was such commotion as could rarely have been heard in a house of worship; and at the fourth I heard my own voice join the rest. As from a distance I could hear the voices of the other two ministers, but what they said, or what took place for the scant rest of the service, I did not know. When I recovered my senses I was halfway home, being pulled along by a grim, striding John Proctor, with Elizabeth and the children hurrying close behind.

Bleak January moved into frigid February, and by an unspoken agreement Ingersoll's ordinary became our meeting place. Ever since that day when Abby had insisted we needed no help from Tituba, and had proved it by seeing Satan, Tituba had looked upon us with disapproval.

"You children be mixing with something too much for you," she told us. "You is playing with hellfire, and it going to burn you."

"But, Tituba," Abby reminded her, "'twas you who first taught us things. You read our palms, and told our fortunes with your cards."

"And I warned you! You 'member, Abigail? I warned you about big black trouble!"

"But we are not in any trouble, Tituba!"

"It be hanging right over your heads! I can see it!"

So it was Abby who first preferred Ingersoll's, where there were always people eager to watch and marvel at us, rather than the familiar keeping room at the Parris house, where Tituba's frown became deeper and deeper.

John might have forbidden me to join the others at Ingersoll's, but he did not. He seemed now to pay no attention to what we did nor what the villagers said of us.

"I have better things to do than bother with the ridiculous carryings-on of a handful of hysterical young females," he announced to Mistress Proctor. "Let them rid themselves of these antics and come back to their proper minds, and, please God, let it be soon!"

And stubbornly I told myself that if John had cared aught for me he would have kept me away from the others, kept me safe at home. Since he did not care, I would go as I chose! At Ingersoll's, surrounded by the other girls, I had a place of my own—a place of importance! People paid us attention!

There were days when we simply sat in the tavern, talking quietly together, nibbling on a piece of Sarah Ingersoll's spicy gingerbread, giggling a bit as young girls are wont to do. And then there were days when—oh, how can I tell it—when one of us began to feel that overpowering urge to move, to seek the release of small sounds, of moans, or small guttural barks. And the small sounds would grow, and other voices would join, and the movements became violent, and we would lose ourselves in our own actions, barely hearing the awed comments from those who watched us, barely hearing that whispered word, *possessed.*

And from these takings we emerged feeling refreshed, and ready to accept the cosseting and comfort that was lavished upon us. We were the center of interest in Salem Village, and even had we chosen to give up the mischief it was far too late. That became clear on the afternoon that Anne Putnum clapped her hands to her thin legs, hidden by her skirts.

"Oh," she screamed, and her voice was filled with pain. "Oh! I am being pinched! Don't! Don't! Stop! Oh, my legs!"

And then, at last and openly, the evil word *witch* joined the sibilant word *possessed.*

"Possessed by witches," the villagers murmured. "The poor children! But who? Who are the witches? Witches here in Salem Village?"

And there was no answer. Not then.

Mary Walcott's aunt, Mistress Mary Sibley, claimed she knew of a test that would identify a witch, and quietly sought out Tituba to discuss it. I do not know what was said, but they must have laid their plans secretly, since Goody Sibley admitted later it was a test that would not be sanctioned by any church or minister, and it was arranged for a day when Samuel Parris would be away from home.

We were bidden to gather once again in the Parris keeping room, and as some of us passed by Ingersoll's on our way, I saw old Goody Good standing by the tavern door, her reeking pipe in her mouth, watching us closely. Beside her, ancient and ailing Goody Osburne stood, leaning heavily on her stick, and the two old crones mumbled together as they saw us go past. Both women were looked down upon by the villagers, Goody Good because of her begging and her filthy appearance, Goody Osburne because she was said to have taken William Osburne to her bed long before she wed him. So they stood alone, those two, and watched us enter the Parris house, and we closed the heavy door on their curious faces.

Mistress Sibley was there with Tituba and John Indian, who was holding a hungry-looking small dog by a rope. Wide-eyed and uneasy, we seated ourselves on the stools and settles as Goody Sibley rolled up her sleeves in the heat of the blazing fire and spoke briskly.

"If so be in truth you poor children are possessed by witches," she said, "then 'twere well to find these creatures and have an end to the trouble!" She nodded at Mary Walcott, who sat, eyes downcast, working on her knitting. "My poor niece is so often taken with great spasms of her body and wild imaginings of her mind that I tremble for her health, and so it must be with all of you. So let us try to spy out those who harm you with their black powers, so we may all return to peace."

She picked up a small blue bowl and, without changing her crisp tone, went on. "Now, here in this bowl I have rye meal, and I am going to mix it with urine from all of you children."

Our eyes flew to Goody Sibley's face. "What?" gasped Anne Putnum.

The woman nodded calmly. "Betake yourselves to the small shed behind this room and make use of the chamber pot you will find there. I will wait."

By twos and threes, red-faced, we left the keeping room for the frigid cold of the shed, following instructions, hurrying back to the warmth as soon as we could. As I resumed my seat on one of the long settles I glanced at Abigail, who was opposite me on the other side of the hearth. She sat demurely, ankles crossed, hands folded in her lap, her head lowered, but I could see her expression, and with shock I realized she was doing all she could to keep from laughing aloud. For myself, I was terrified. There seemed an unholy air about what we were doing, smacking of what little I had heard of conjuring and black magic.

When the last girl returned from the shed, Mistress Sibley handed John Indian a wooden dipper and bade him fill it from the chamber pot. He looked uneasily at Tituba, who nodded to him slightly. John handed her the end of the little dog's rope and left the room.

In the few seconds that he was gone none of us spoke. My eyes wandered to a window, and I could see Goody Good and Goody Osburne outside, craning as if trying to observe what we were up to. If they but knew!

John returned, holding the filled dipper well away from himself, and handed it to Goody Sibley, who poured a small amount into the bowl of rye meal. Using a spoon, she mixed it well, and then shaped it into a small cake and laid it in the hot ashes on the edge of the fire. As though we were expecting some toothsome treat she said smoothly, "It should not take long to bake."

As we sat there, silent, there came a small tapping on the outer door, and I knew it must be the two old women, Good and Osburne, hoping to come in and see for themselves what was taking place. Throwing a shawl about her shoulders, Tituba opened the door, said a few quiet words to the women outside, and then went out, closing the door behind her.

We tried to make conversation, but the room seemed wrapped in stillness. Presently Goody Sibley poked at the cake with a long fork and declared it done. Spearing it with the fork, she waved it from side to side, letting it cool slightly.

"Now," she said to John Indian, "free the dog."

John untied the rope from about the dog's scrawny neck, and Mistress Sibley held the cake out to it. The poor beast must have been half-starved, for after one inquisitive sniff it gulped the cake down with apparent pleasure. My stomach heaved at the thought!

We sat staring at the dog, at Mistress Sibley, at John Indian, waiting for something to happen. Goody Sibley smiled at us.

"The little dog will tell us who the witches are," she said. "You will see!"

A moment later the door opened and Tituba entered, followed by Goody Good, mouthing her noisome pipe, and Goody Osburne, leaning heavily upon her stick. The dog turned toward the sound of the opening door, ears pricked forward. In a moment of impatience Tituba made a shooing motion with her hand and bade the animal to "get you gone!" Goody Good snickered around her pipe, and Mistress Osburne lifted her stick to lay it aside. Perhaps believing it was about to be thrashed, the dog lifted its lip in a snarl, crouched back, and began to growl. The short hairs on its back bristled; its teeth were bared. John Indian moved to the door and opened it again. Sidling around the three women, the beast tucked its tail between its legs and bolted.

"So!" said Mistress Sibley. "So! 'Tis you! You three are the witches!"

We stared at each other, bewildered. Betty Parris lifted her arms toward Tituba, that warm loving slave who had so often held and petted her.

"Tituba!" she cried. "Not my Tituba!"

Then she fell to the floor in a deep swoon, whilst the rest of us sat white-faced and shaken.

# SEVEN

THE WORD SPREAD like fire in a thatched roof, and the names of Tituba, Goody Good, and Goody Osburne were flung from end to end of Salem Village. They could not have been better chosen. Tituba was of a different color, came from a distant and unknown land, and even spoke in a manner unlike the villagers, her voice being softer and more musical to the ear. 'Twas well known, too, that she could read palms and tell the tarot cards, and had, in fact, done so for many of the women. Certainly these things should be considered.

As for Goody Good, everything about her fitted the concept of a witch—her begging, her curt, rough speech, her slovenly, unkempt appearance, her pipe. The naming of Goody Good roused little surprise.

And Goody Osburne's unseemly behavior with her hired man had put her into disfavor with most of the village. Nor had she been to Sabbath meeting in many weeks, though I think she could not be blamed, since once there she was ignored by everyone.

In any case, these three were accepted by Salem Village as the cause of our fits and pains and babblings, and Reverend Parris, overlooking the manner in which the naming had been done, now joined with John Hale and Nicholas Noyes in questioning us. Since we had not made the accusations it seemed easier now to accept them. Anne admitted that she had known 'twas Goody Good who pinched her, but had been "afeared to say the name." Abigail confessed that she, too, had been pinched by Goody Good.

"And Goody Osburne was with her and scratched me, but I dared not tell," she added.

And those respected men of the cloth hung upon our every word, so that we tried to satisfy them. But little was said of Tituba. In truth, we did not dare. She may have been the one to set our minds on this strange road, but only because of our coaxing. She had disapproved of us, she had warned us, and we had not listened. And by her own word Tituba knew more of witchcraft than she had ever revealed to us.

But though we might hold our tongues regarding her, others did not. To the people of Salem Village, Tituba was their choice for a witch, and they made it known on the twenty-ninth day of February, that day which, with its own magic, comes only once every four years. Formal complaints were sworn out and warrants were issued for Mistress Good, Mistress Osburne, and Tituba. All three were taken to Ipswich Prison to await an examination of the evidence against them.

With Tituba gone from the Parris house Betty appeared to draw into herself until she could scarce be reached by word nor touch. It no longer took the flickering flames nor the stillness of water to send her wide eyes staring into space; she spent most of her time that way. She slept poorly, had no appetite, lost her soft rosiness. She was listless and spoke rarely, and often would sit sobbing quietly with no seeming cause. Her mother, more free of her racking cough now that the early days of spring brought a mildness in the weather, tried to tempt her with food, tried to rouse her interest in daily living, tried to soothe her into sleep. But it had been a long time since Mistress Parris had devoted attention to her daughter. Her place had been filled by Tituba, and with Tituba absent, no one and nothing could reach the child.

As for the rest of us, we could go to any extremes of behavior, secure in the knowledge that we were "possessed." We could name our tormentors as we cowered in corners or under the furniture—"I see the shape of Goody Good! She tries to burn me with her pipe!" As we writhed on the floor of Ingersoll's ordinary it was because "Goody Osburne is sticking needles into me!" As we screamed and shrieked and ran about the room, always filled with onlookers, we cried that one witch or another was "trying to get her hands on my throat!"

And if it was often Abigail, though sometimes Anne Putnum, who began these fits, they were swiftly joined by the rest of us. It was nigh to impossible to witness these explosions of released emotion without feeling oneself slide into them. When one girl screeched, in a moment we all screeched. When one girl threw herself to the floor and rolled in apparent agony, so did we all. When one saw the "shape" of witches, they were visible to each of us. We were caught. Frightened, bewildered, confused, but caught, in a coil of our own making.

If, sometimes, I was able to withhold myself from their takings, able to sit with my hands clenched tight together and my teeth clamped against the jerking and the screaming that invaded me, it was only with the most supreme, exhausting force of will. To be there, wherever we poor "possessed" girls were, was to share in the hysteria.

Then why did I go to Ingersoll's almost daily?

How could I not?

I suppose it is natural for young girls to rebel against the strictures of older women, who seem never to recall when they, too, felt the rioting juices of youth. Some mothers may look upon their daughters and think, "Ah, yes. I remember how it was to be that young." But the mistress of a bound girl does not, nor do other unrelated persons. And this may be part of the reason why those we named as witches—and God help us, how many there were!—were never the parents of those of us fortunate enough to have such. But with the others we were ruthless. It is but rarely that youth has power over its elders, and power is a heady brew.

It was on a Tuesday, the first day of March, when the sky was spring blue and the air had a softness in it, that hearings were held for Goody Good, Goody Osburne, and Tituba. I think there was not a soul in Salem Village who was not there, and many had come from the small towns around us, Beverly and Ipswich, Lynn and Topsfield. At first it was thought to have the hearings in Ingersoll's ordinary, but the size of the gathering made that impossible. Instead the excited audience, wet-lipped with anticipation, was herded into the church, where the ten of us "poor possessed children" were seated together in a place of honor. Reverend Parris's tall chair was turned about for the accused to stand upon and be well viewed, and a long table was set before it. Here sat one Ezekial Cheever as secretary, and the two magistrates, John Hathorne and Jonathan Corwin.

Sarah Good was led into the room.

Ragged, underfed, and scorned as she might be, that day she seemed uncaring of Salem Village's opinion of her. With a firm step she walked to the chair, clambered up on it, and stood, chin high, pipe in her mouth, surveying the assembly with a sparkle in her eye. It was but rarely, if ever, that Goody Good could have stood above the crowd with every eye upon her, every ear pricked to hear what she might say.

It was John Hathorne who spoke first, and his deep voice seemed to savor the words.

"Sarah Good, what evil spirit have you familiarity with?"

Goody Good looked down at him. "None!" she said shortly.

"Have you made no contract with the Devil?"

"No."

"Why do you hurt these children?"

Goody Good stared at each of us, taking her time. At last she said, "I do not hurt them. I scorn it!"

Magistrate Hathorne rose from his chair and walked deliberately to Mistress Good. Standing beside her, he put his hands behind his back beneath his coattails, gazing at the ten of us, sitting demurely in a row, our eyes on our folded hands.

"Children," he said, "I ask you now to look upon Sarah Good. Look well, and tell us if this is the person who has hurt and tormented you!"

With the others I raised my eyes and stared at that dirty, wrinkled face, the same face I had seen so many times in the village. Shrewish, stench-ridden, a nuisance to the town— but, witch?

Beside me Anne Putnum lifted her voice in a shriek, Abigail Williams fell to the floor and lay there writhing, little Betty Parris stiffened in her chair and beat her head against its high back, Mary Walcott threw herself down beside Abigail—and I? And I? My heart breaks to tell it, but my voice joined the rest. And throughout the crowded room there ran a sound like the escape of a long-held breath. This was what the audience had come to see.

Hathorne's strong voice rang out above the clamor.

"Sarah Good, do you not see now what you have done? Why do you not tell us the truth? Why do you torment these poor children?"

The old woman's voice was shrill. "I do not torment

them! You bring others here, and now you charge me with it!"

Question and answer, the voices rose hotly against each other.

"We brought you here—"

"But you brought in two more—"

"Who was it then that tormented the children?"

"It was Osburne!"

We had quieted, and now as the magistrate faced us and we looked back at him, breathing quickly after our exertions, I felt—and I believe the others did, too—exhilarated and cleansed.

"Tell us, children, and be not afraid to speak the truth —is it Sarah Good who torments you?"

Mercy Lewis's slow voice came first. "'Tis both, sir. Goody Good and Goody Osburne both."

"They afflict us sorely," Elizabeth Booth cried out. "They hurt and torment us!"

"'Tis their shapes that come," Abigail said. "'Tis no matter where their bodies are, be they in Ipswich jail or in their own homes! 'Tis their shapes that fly at us through doors and windows!"

"Their shapes, aye, their shapes! If we touch them there is nothing there!" That was Susanna Sheldon, covering her eyes as if to keep out a fearsome sight.

"But they touch us." Anne Putnum's voice was calm. "They pinch us, and pull our hair. They stick us with needles and reach for our throats to strangle us."

"Hah!" said Sarah Good, and she spat on the floor,

barely missing the sleeve of John Hathorne's coat. Quickly, and with scant ceremony, Goody Good was led from the room. In a few moments Goody Osburne took her place.

Elderly and unwell, she was a pitiable creature, but there was little pity in the faces of those who stared up at her. Leaning heavily upon the high back of Reverend Parris's chair, her voice a-quaver, she answered much the same questions as had been put to Goody Good.

No, she was not familiar with any evil spirit. No, she made no contract with the Devil. No, she had never hurt these children, nor any others, in her life.

"What familiarity have you with Sarah Good?" asked Hathorne.

"None."

"Where did you last see her?"

"One day, a-going to town."

"Sarah Good saith that it was you that hurt the children."

The woman's voice trembled even more. "I do not know that the Devil goes about in my likeness to do any hurt."

And then again we were asked to stand and look upon Goody Osburne, and say if we did know her, and then again came our voices, telling of the mischief she had done us. And when we were finished John Hathorne smiled at his success, and Goody Osburne was led away.

We knew, all of us, who was to come next. If there was one who might, in truth, be a witch, it was surely Tituba. What powers had she? What might she do to us? How could we protect ourselves? And so it was that the moment Tituba came through the door we immediately fell into such a taking that nothing could be heard above the noise we made.

But Tituba was wise. If telling the truth, as Goody Good and Goody Osburne had done, was to be disbelieved, then she would spin the tales this roomful of listeners wanted to hear. In spite of ourselves we hushed lest we miss some part of what she said.

"Who is it hurts these children?"

Tituba's voice, soft, low, musical, made everyone strain to hear her. "The Devil, for aught I know."

"Did you never see the Devil?"

"The Devil came to me, and bid me serve him."

A sigh drifted over the room, and we, in our seats below Tituba, leaned back easily in our chairs, our eyes fastened on her calm face, a sense of peace flowing through us as she told her story—the story that Salem Village wanted to accept.

Four women sometimes hurt the children, Tituba told them—Goody Osburne and Goody Good, and two others whom she did not know. They had wanted her to hurt the children also, but she would not until they promised to hurt her much more badly if she refused.

And then she spoke of a little black man—"Hairy like a beast, he is, but goes upright like a man"—and a tall man from Boston, who came to her demanding that she harm us. "He came with Goody Osburne," Tituba said calmly.

"This tall man from Boston. What clothes doth he go in?"

"He goes in black clothes. A tall man, with white hair, I think. He brought with him a book."

"What sort of book?"

"The Devil's book. He wanted me to sign."

"Were there other names in the book?"

"Aye. Goody Good. Her name was there. And Osburne, too."

"How many names were there?"

"There were nine names."

A gasp went up from those assembled. Nine names! Then—why, then the end had not come with the arrest of the three women! There were others, other witches, and the tall man himself. And the little black man! The hunt must go on!

With determination Magistrate Hathorne resumed his questioning, and Tituba continued her story. She told of a great black dog that appeared to her, saying, "Serve me," and that when she replied that she was afraid, the dog threatened hideous punishments did she not obey. She spoke of a red cat and a black cat, of a hog, and of a yellow bird that was always with the "tall man from Boston." She spoke of riding upon sticks through the air.

"Do you go over the trees or through them?"

"We see nothing, but are there presently," said Tituba.

"Did you not pinch Elizabeth Hubbard this morning?" demanded Hathorne.

"The tall man brought her to me and made me pinch her."

"Why did you go to Thomas Putnum's last night and hurt his child?"

"They pull and haul me and make me go."

"And what would they have you do?"

"Kill her with a knife."

"Why did you not tell your master?"

"I was afraid. They said they would cut off my head if I told."

"What attendants hath Sarah Good?"

"A yellow bird, and she would have given me one."

"What food did she give it?"

"It did suck between her fingers."

At that there was a sudden gasp from the listeners, who had hung upon each quiet word. 'Twas well known that a yellow bird was one of the Devil's recognized associates, and common knowledge that one way to prove a witch was by any small growth upon her body, for it was by means of these unholy teats that witches suckled their familiars, those creatures—whatever they might be, cats, rats, dogs, or birds —that did the bidding of their masters. Even John Hathorne's eyes narrowed as if he were searching Tituba's body for a similar excrescence, but he continued quickly in his questioning lest this fountain of information run dry.

"A yellow bird," he repeated. "And what hath Sarah Osburne?"

"Yesterday she had a thing with a head like a woman, with two legs and wings."

Instantly Abigail's voice rose clearly in the whispering room. "Aye," she said. "I have seen that creature, and it turned into the shape of Goody Osburne."

Anne Putnum nodded solemnly, her eyes wide, and without thinking the rest of us nodded with her. I could see Ezekial Cheever, the secretary, his nose close to the paper, his eyes darting about the room to note all our actions, writing as rapidly as he could with his long quill pen, the tip of his tongue showing between his lips.

The questioning went on and on, and shocked satisfaction was on every face. A confessed witch, one who had shared words with Satan, one who had flown upon her stick above the trees, one who was telling them all the secrets of that frightening, hideous, black nether world—this was what they wanted.

Tituba's melodic voice seemed almost to chant her responses. I felt lulled and calm, and I began to see clearly the things of which she spoke. That tall man dressed in black with his Devil's book was real to me. The yellow bird, suckling obscenely between Sarah Good's fingers. The red cats, the black ones, the hog, the dog. The woman's shape with wings that Abby said had turned into Goody Osburne's shape. I, too, could see it. If Tituba spoke of these things then they must be so, for her voice wrapped me round as a blanket might swaddle an infant, her words drifted into my mind and settled there. Something far stronger than I had moved into me until I felt at peace, with no will of my own. And if such a feeling had come real to me, then surely that band of girls surrounding me must feel the same. If Tituba had been labeled witch, then we had become the witch's children.

It seemed as if from a distance that I heard John Hathorne's final words. "Who is it hurts these children now?"

But Tituba, now that she had told of her alliance with the Devil, thus betraying him, could see no more of his fiendish works. Her voice seemed weary when she answered. "I am blind now. I cannot see."

She was led from the room, and only then did I realize that Betty Parris had sat silent through Tituba's hearing, her eyes fixed emptily on space.

Within a short time the three women were removed to the prison in Boston, there to await a formal trial.

# EIGHT

If Tituba had not said there were nine names written in the Devil's book, would it all have been over then? Would the people of Salem Village have gone into their fields to prepare them for the spring planting, as John Proctor, removing himself as far as possible from the unease that was everywhere, proceeded to do? Could we have put an end then to our exhibitions? Or were we truly possessed by black power? Today, so much later, I still do not know.

In the early March days that followed the imprisonment of Tituba, Goody Good, and Goody Osburne, we were frequently called together by whatever men of the law or the church chose to question us. John Hathorne and Jonathan Corwin, Reverend Parris and Reverend Hale and Reverend Noyes, all of them spent time with us, asking, demanding, pleading.

"Who afflicts thee?" we were asked time and again. "Who is the cause of your pain and distress? What tall man from Boston hath appeared to thee? Hast there been a hairy little black man?" But none of these questions could we answer.

""'Tis your duty to aid us in searching out this evil," we were told. "Look deep into yourselves, use this power that God hath seen fit to give you, and tell us the names of those you see."

And we lowered our eyes in modest fashion and said little.

Betty Parris said least of all. She became increasingly pale and nervous, and wept when the ministers and magistrates spoke to her, no matter how gently. At home she barely touched her food and tossed restlessly at night, arising with dark hollow eyes and shaking hands. That first week in March Mistress Parris sent Betty off to stay with family friends, the Stephen Sewalls, in Salem Town, a few miles from the village. If Reverend Parris preferred to keep his small daughter at home where he could watch and pray over her, dislodging the evil spirits from her frail body, he was unable to convince his wife. So Betty was taken from the group, and would to God the same had been done for all of us!

As for the nine of us left, Abigail Williams became our leader. When Abby chose to spend a few hours at Ingersoll's, most of us joined her. If she was stricken of a sudden and moaned in pain, we felt the same agony. We saw dim shapes around us, but could see no faces and so, for a while, we could name no names.


""'Tis a pity you cannot put as much energy into your work about my house as you put into your antics at Ingersoll's," John Proctor said to me one evening as we sat at supper. "I hear you and your friends become more violent each day."

His words hurt. I faced him angrily. "But can you not see that we suffer?" I snapped.

"If you suffer it is by your own doing. To have named as witch two helpless women, and a third most likely because her skin is black, to have done that is evil mischief. May it all fall upon your own heads!"

I was unable to keep the tears from my eyes. Mistress Proctor laid her hand gently over mine.

"Thee must not speak so of our Mary, John. What she does is by no will of her own."

"Then 'tis time she had a will of her own rather than aping the madness of those she calls friends!" He raised the knife he held and pointed it at me. "Left to themselves," he said, his deep eyes boring into mine, "these girls will make devils of us all!" And he threw down the knife, rose from the table, and left.

Elizabeth Proctor tried to soothe me. "John speaks only from concern for you," she said. "He feels you do harm to yourself, and it distresses him. Try to understand, child."

But I could not. I wanted strength and comfort from him, not blame and doubt.


Friday, the eleventh of March, was declared by the various ministers as a day of fasting and prayer in Salem Village, a day of bringing God's attention to the little town and the misery that had befallen it. The local folk gathered in the meetinghouse, where first one man of God and then another beseeched the Almighty to look upon us, his poor possessed children, and give us the strength to name our tormentors. The voices went on and on, the pleading rose, there was the constant small rustle of assenting words from the townspeople. Suddenly Anne Putnum lifted her thin hand and pointed upward to the strong beams that held the roof.

"There!" she screamed. "There—on that beam—there she sits! Do you see her? A witch! A witch! Martha Cory is a witch!"

The villagers sat stunned. Martha Cory? That respectable woman? A woman who, like John Proctor, had expressed great skepticism about our fits? A constant attender of church services? Not Martha Cory! Her absence that day was her undoing.

On the following morning Anne's uncle, Edward Putnum, and Ezekial Cheever paid a visit to Martha Cory. Before they left they talked with Anne.

"Can you see Goody Cory's shape, Anne? Is it clear to you?"

Anne, eyes tightly closed, shook her head. "No," she said, "I see nothing."

"Cannot you see what her shape is wearing? How is she clothed? We want no errors here."

The words of Tituba were graven in Anne's mind. "I am blind now," she told them. "I cannot see."

Her Uncle Edward's voice was gentle. "Why can you not see, Anne? Why are you blind?"

"Martha Cory hath blinded me. She knows that you come to her to accuse her. She knows that I named her. She hath blinded me."

Reluctantly the two men paid their call on Goody Cory, prepared perhaps at first to keep their minds open. They were met by an amused woman who laughed at their questions, and then turned serious.

"'Twould serve your purpose better," she snapped at them, "were you to stop the mouths of the scandalmongers. Talk is loose in Salem Village, and well ye know it! Stop the talk and you will stop this nonsense!"

Ezekial Cheever was shocked. "You call it nonsense, ma'am, when already three witches have been named?"

"'Tis a long mile between the naming and the truth," Martha Cory said. "For me, I do not believe in witches!"

In Salem Village such words were the greatest blasphemy. If there was God and His angels—and who would deny that?—then it followed that there was the Devil and his witches. To believe or disbelieve in one was to believe or disbelieve in both. And if one did not believe in God, it must be because one had sided with Satan.

On Saturday, March 19, a warrant was sworn out for Martha Cory's arrest, but since the next day was the Sabbath, delivery of the warrant was put off until the Monday.

In the meantime a former resident of Salem Village returned to town.

# NINE

BEFORE SAMUEL PARRIS had been appointed minister to Salem Village, the post had been held by one Deodat Lawson, who had later been called to a more important church in Boston. In recent weeks Lawson had received confusing and confused letters from such fellow clergymen as Reverend Parris, Reverend Hale, and Reverend Noyes, begging him to return and aid them in hunting down unnamed witches. Witches in quiet little Salem Village? Lawson must have felt an amused incredulity on that Saturday, March 19, as his horse clopped down the familiar dusty road. Dismounting at Ingersoll's ordinary to refresh himself, he pushed open the heavy door and may well have thought he was entering into Hell.

A few candles, added to the reddish glow of the low fire on the hearth, laid flickering shadows across white faces that lined the room, all watching a figure that twisted and screamed upon the floor. Deodat Lawson stopped short.

"What ails the female?" he demanded of the nearest face. "Who is she? Why does no one help her?"

"'Tis Mary Walcott, Reverend, Mistress Sibley's niece. She says a witch has bitten her."

"A witch? Here? And did no one see it happen?"

"Oh, we never see them, Reverend. Only the possessed girls see them. And then they claim to see only the shapes of the witches. Thank God you have come, sir! 'Tis a fearsome thing, not knowing which of our neighbors is a witch!"

Taking a candle from its socket on the tavern wall, Lawson strode to the girl and knelt beside her, his cloak swirling out about him.

"Mary," he said firmly. "Mary Walcott!"

At the unfamiliar voice Mary stopped her screams and opened her eyes, staring up at him. "I do not know you," she murmured.

"That matters not. Show me where a witch hath bitten thee."

Her eyes fastened on his face, Mary slowly pushed back one sleeve of her gown, holding her arm out to him. "There," she said. "She bit me there."

"Hmm," said Deodat Lawson.

From the circle of dim faces came questions. "Are there marks on her arm, Reverend? Can you see the marks of witch's teeth?"

The minister spoke cautiously. "There is a red mark of some sort," he admitted. "What may have caused it I could not say."

And who could blame Reverend Lawson if the thought ran through his mind that Mary might well have inflicted the slight wound with her own teeth? In any case he helped her to her feet, noting, as others had done, that she seemed none the worse for her experience, and then retired thoughtfully to the taproom.

It was evening when he arrived at Samuel Parris's home, and he was surprised at the number of villagers who had gathered there. Anne Putnum sat close to Abigail, both of them deep in a whispered conversation.

After quick introductions Reverend Parris led Lawson into the small, chilly room that served as his study, closing the door firmly behind them. In the keeping room the talk moved to whether Reverend Lawson would be able to identify the children's tormentors.

"He saw where Mary Walcott were bitten at Ingersoll's," someone said. "That should be proof enough."

"Aye, for some of us 'tis more proof, did we need it, but Reverend Lawson comes late to our trouble. He knows naught of what Salem Village has seen. Even for us 'twere hard to believe in the beginning."

"Do the Reverend bide here a bit, he will believe!"

"Mayhap, but recall the Reverend were ever a cautious man."

Slowly Abigail laid down her sewing, and rose to her feet. Then, as if blown by some gigantic wind, she whirled once around the keeping room, dashed out, and ran along the corridor to the study, flinging open the door. Arms flapping wildly, narrow eyes glassy bright, she darted into the room, bringing both men to their feet.

"Whish!" she shouted. "Whish! Whish! I am going to fly!" Circling the small room, she rushed out again and her racing steps could be heard running up the stairs and down, through the keeping room, back into the study and out again.

The two men followed her to the study door, gazing after her.

"You see?" Parris said helplessly. "This is the way things are. I know not where to turn."

In the keeping room those who heard him nodded their heads in sympathy, and then listened as Deodat Lawson's voice came clearly.

"But surely, Samuel, it could be mischief. Play-acting. A mere child trying to draw attention to herself. Flying, indeed!"

From the keeping room Abigail's voice rose in a ringing scream. "I won't! I won't! Oh, help me! Help me!"

The two reverends reached the keeping-room door to see Abby thrusting her arms out before her as if trying to hold off some pressing force. Around her hovered the villagers, eagerly watching Lawson to see how he would respond to this behavior that had become so familiar to them.

Anne Putnum stood in shadow, her back against the wall, hands clasped tightly. Her eyes were fastened on Abby, and her lips seemed to be framing two words, repeating them silently over and over.

As if wrestling with Satan himself, Abby fought wildly, beating with clenched fists against the empty air, as Anne cowered, watching. Mistress Elizabeth Parris moved toward her niece.

"Abby! Abby, child! What is it? What frightens you?"

"Do you not see her?" Abby shrieked. "Why, there she

stands! Oh no, I won't! I won't!" Her cap loosened and fell, her hair tangled as she shook her head violently from side to side. "I won't! I am sure it is none of God's book! It is the Devil's book for all I know!"

Suddenly she dashed to the fireplace and snatched a burning brand from the low flames, waving it before her. "Go! Go! I will not sign the book!" Hurling the brand into a corner of the room, she ran back and grasped more, throwing them helter-skelter. There was sudden movement as people twitched their garments from the small fires, stamped to put them out, or managed to toss them back into the great fireplace. Like a terrified animal Abigail panted and fought until with one last wail she sank to the floor, barely conscious. Deodat Lawson bent down to her.

"Who was it, Abigail? Tell us whom you saw."

But it was Anne Putnum's voice that answered from the shadows by the wall. "And did you not see her then? 'Twas a shape. The shape of Rebecca Nurse."

Closeted again with Samuel Parris, Reverend Lawson made his disbelief plain.

"It's impossible, Sam! I knew Mistress Nurse well when I served here, and there could be no one more Christian and devout than she! An old, old woman, deaf and filled with the aches of age, loved by every member of that large family she has raised. No, Sam, I can't believe it!"

"And yet you saw Abigail fighting as if for her very life! Could you doubt that?"

"Aye, I watched her, Sam, and I confess I know not what

to make of it. The child seemed terrified—seemed, in truth, to be battling some evil force. But that the force was Goody Nurse—that, my friend, I cannot credit!"

Reverend Lawson was not the only one. Certainly the name flew about the village, but in every case it aroused doubt.

On the next day, however, the Sunday, there was fresh food for consideration for all those who appeared at the church meeting, and who, in all of Salem Village, did not? Even Martha Cory was there! Since the warrant had not yet been served for her arrest she was free to come and go as she chose, and, intrepid woman that she was, she chose to attend church. To all appearances she sat stolid and quiet, paying no attention to the whispered remarks, the staring and pointing of those around her. But as the services began it became apparent that, though Martha Cory might be there in the flesh, causing no trouble, behaving as any churchgoer should, the shape of Martha Cory was at work amongst us.

At first our twitchings and cowerings were slight, but presently Abigail, then Anne, then the rest of us cried out as we had done so often before.

With an effort the Reverend Lawson, asked to conduct the service, did his best to lift his voice above our shriller ones, and words of his prayer rang through our clamor. Then Abigail jumped to her feet.

"Look!" she cried. "There sits Goody Cory on the beam, suckling a yellow bird between her fingers!"

Even as I knew the words to be those that Tituba had

used against Sarah Good, so, as truly, did it seem that I could see the shape of Martha Cory upon the beam. With the others I pointed. Anne Putnum rose quickly and stepped forward.

"There is the bird," she said clearly. "It flies from the beam now, now it perches on Reverend Lawson's hat— there, where it hangs on the peg."

It was her father's strong hand that pulled Anne back into her seat, and we said no more. But we had said enough.

On Monday morning Martha Cory took her place, as had others before her, on the minister's chair in the meeting-house. Her hands tied loosely together, she stood straight, looking down at us with scornful eyes.

Magistrate Hathorne opened the questioning. "You are now in the hands of authority," he said. "Tell me now why you hurt these persons."

Mistress Cory's words were strong and clear. "I do not!"

"Who doth?"

And just as strongly, "Pray, give me leave to go to prayer."

"We do not send for you to go to prayer," said Hathorne sternly. "Tell me why you hurt these." A broad gesture of his arm indicated the row where we all sat silently.

"I am an innocent person," Goody Cory announced. "I never had to do with witchcraft since I was born. I am a gospel woman."

"She's a gospel *witch*!" one of us cried out, and in an instant the rest took up the chant. "Gospel witch! Gospel witch!"

No one could speak through the noise we made, until suddenly Anne Putnum jumped up. "Goody Cory prays to the Devil," she said. "When in my father's house I saw her shape, hers and another's. They were praying to the Devil. That is where Goody Cory's prayers go!"

Abigail's voice came next. "Look!" she commanded. "Look now! The tall man from Boston whispers in her ear! Do you not see?"

Immediately Hathorne spoke. "What did he say to you?" he demanded of Goody Cory.

Her head held high, the woman answered. "We must not believe all that these distracted children say."

But Hathorne was insistent. "Cannot you tell what that man whispered?"

"I saw nobody," Mistress Cory answered, and bit her lip.

Immediately all of us bit ours, Mercy Lewis until the blood came.

"See you now," said Hathorne, "as you bite your lip, so do they theirs."

"What harm is there in it?" asked Mistress Cory calmly.

Unexpectedly John Hathorne ordered that her hands be untied. As the knot was loosened the woman flexed her fingers.

Abigail sprang from her seat, rubbing her arm. "Goody Cory hath pinched me," she cried out.

Immediately we were all a-twitch and a-scream until the magistrates retied Martha Cory's hands. Instantly we were quiet.

"Do you not see these children are rational and sober as their neighbors when your hands are fastened?" he said to her.

The woman simply stared at him coldly and shifted her feet a bit on the chair. At once all our feet were shifting and stamping on the board floor.

Facing the woman squarely, his voice lifted above the thunder of our moving feet, John Hathorne spoke. "What do you say to all these things that are apparent?"

And angrily, Mistress Cory answered him. "If you will all go hang me, how can I help it?"

Presently Goody Cory was released from the chair and led from the room. Her husband, Giles, an old and slow-witted man who knew little beyond the demands of a farmer's life, was brought in. He seemed anxious to do correctly whatever was expected of him.

Could he, the magistrates wanted to know, give any instances when his wife's behavior might be considered as that of a witch? The man's furrowed brow wrinkled even more, and he scratched his thick hair, almost white, with gnarled fingers. 'Twas hard to say, he muttered. He knew little of witches, he was a churchgoing man. But there had been that day. . .

"Sometime last week, I fetched an ox out of the woods about noon. He lay down in the yard and I went to raise him, to yoke him to the plow, but he could not rise. He dragged his hinder parts, as if he had been hip-shot. Then Martha came out to see what was the trouble, and then the ox did rise." He gazed about him as if to see whether he had said the right thing.

"And has there been aught else?" Hathorne asked.

Again Cory scratched his head, struggling to find some answer. "I had a cat, strangely taken on the sudden, and it did make me think she would have died presently. My wife bid me knock her in the head, but I did not, and since, she is well."

"Ah," said Hathorne.

Old Cory's face lighted as if with sudden inspiration. "My wife hath been wont to sit up after I went to bed, and I have perceived her to kneel down by the hearth, as if she were at prayer, but heard nothing." He smiled about him, obviously, in his poor, blundering way, hoping he had said something to please the awesome authorities.

"And did you think she was praying to Satan?" Hathorne asked.

Giles Cory looked puzzled. "And why would Martha do that? Martha is a gospel woman."

And again, on the instant, came our chant, "Gospel witch! Gospel witch!"

And so Martha Cory, too, was taken off to the jail that already housed Sarah Good, Sarah Osburne, and Tituba. A few days later, without the benefit of a hearing, since it was felt 'twould not do for someone so young, little Dorcas

Good, four years of age, was taken to join them. Her shape, Abigail had said, ran about the village like a small mad dog, biting us, the possessed, because of our accusations against her mother. Perhaps Dorcas did not mind so much. She would certainly have been better fed in prison than by the scant bits of food given her by the frugal people of Salem Village.

# TEN

THOSE WERE SUCH frightening weeks! I seemed to have lost my own will. I could not think for myself, nor speak for myself. Whatever the others did, I did also. Our brains, our bodies had become almost as one person, and I could do no more than follow. The nine of us were together most of the time, for the magistrates and the ministers did persist in their questioning of us, and at each questioning new names were mentioned.

John Proctor made it plain that he did not wish me to attend the hearings, but it was demanded that I be there. He stood staring at our little group one day as we waited to enter the meetinghouse, his face grim. Not taking his eyes from us, he spoke to Reverend Lawson, who stood next him.

"They should be at the whipping post," he said. "If they are let to continue their mischief we shall all be devils and witches!"

On the few days that I could stay at home he had barely a word for me. I longed to say to him, "This is not of my doing! I do not know what power has taken me from myself—'tis something too strong for me to pull away. Do not scorn me so. I mean no harm! Speak to me as you used, be gentle with me!" But none of this I ever said. Elizabeth Proctor in her quiet way tried to give me the understanding that John did not, and I turned it away. It was not her comfort I longed for.

Rebecca Nurse might have been a respected member of the little community, but the time had come when there was little respect for anyone in Salem Village—unless it was for us, the possessed children, and the names we threw like bones to hungry dogs. Deodat Lawson, that brave man, insisted that he be one of those to go to Goody Nurse's home and tell her there must be a hearing. I do not know what the poor old woman said when she was told. I know only that she was brought before the magistrates.

Goody Nurse was hard of hearing and so frail with age that Magistrate Hathorne was more kindly toward her than he had been to any of the other accused. Earnestly did he try to make certain she heard each word so that she might answer properly.

"I can say before my eternal Father that I am innocent," Mistress Nurse said, her voice shaking with emotion, "and God will clear my innocence."

"There is never a one in this assembly but desires it," Hathorne replied. And then, his face solemn, he added, "But if you be guilty, I pray God discover you!"

Anne's uncle, Edward Putnum, reported that he had seen his young niece in the throes of physical anguish and that she had screamed, "Rebecca Nurse is torturing me!"

"I am innocent and clear and have not been able to get out of doors these eight-nine days," Goody Nurse retorted. "I never afflicted no child, no, never in my life."

The doubt on Hathorne's face was evident. "Are you then," he asked, "an innocent person relating to this witchcraft?"

Anne Putnum called out, "Did you not bring the tall man from Boston with you? Did you not bid me tempt God and die? How often have you eaten and drunk the bloody sacrament to your own damnation?"

Anne then fell to the floor in a convulsion. The rest of us too were tipped into that same black state, writhing, moaning, and weeping.

John Hathorne turned back to Rebecca Nurse. "What do you say to them?" he demanded.

The old woman stood small in the big chair, her blue-veined hands holding tightly to the back of it, her wide eyes staring at us. "Oh, Lord help me!" she cried.

"It is awful for all to see these agonies," Hathorne said. "To see you stand there with dry eyes when there are so many wet."

"You do not know my heart."

"You would do well if you are guilty to confess."

"Would you have me belie myself?"

And she did not. No matter what was said to Rebecca Nurse, she continued to deny all knowledge and guilt. At last the magistrates ordered her removed. There were tears in Reverend Lawson's eyes as she was led away.

Outside the meetinghouse John Proctor watched the frail old creature being taken to jail, and turned his cold blue eyes on us as we emerged into late afternoon sunlight.

"Hang them! Hang *them*!" he cried, and ignored the shocked disbelief on the faces that turned toward him. He should not have spoken so. We were the poor possessed children. We were the pitied darlings of Salem Village. It was not wise to speak against us.

Oh, John! How could you have done it?

With Tituba in jail her husband, John Indian, worked doubly hard. In the Parris home he did much of the cleaning and some of the cooking that had been Tituba's work, and he continued his work at Ingersoll's tavern. In either place he could watch the behavior of the nine of us, and listen to the gossip and theories of our elders, and certainly it was plain to him that we were the protected pets of the village. Perhaps wise Tituba warned him that to stay aloof could be dangerous when the feelings of others were so aroused. Perhaps the heightened emotions that surrounded him touched some hidden well of island mysteries and superstitions on which he had been raised. Who is there now who can say? In any case, John Indian suddenly shocked us all by testifying against Sarah Cloyce.

Goody Cloyce was the sister of Rebecca Nurse. Wretched and angry after Mistress Nurse's imprisonment, she came to church on April 3, Sacrament Sunday, in the hope, I suppose, that taking the sacrament might comfort her. Her eyes were straight on Reverend Parris when he gave his text. It came from the book of St. John, and the words rang out over the congregation.

*"Have not I chosen you twelve, and one of you is a devil?"*

No sooner were the words uttered than Sarah Cloyce rose to her feet, glared at the preacher, stalked down the aisle, and left the church with a great bang of the door. Over the murmur of surprise and disapproval, the Reverend's next words sparked like lightning.

"Christ knows how many devils there are in His church and who they are!"

At the end of the service, as the church emptied, Elizabeth Booth came out into the sunshine. Suddenly she pointed to a spot on the fresh spring grass.

"See," she cried. "There they gather for their sacrament! The bread is red!"

"And the wine is bloody!" shrieked Susanna Sheldon.

Around us people looked where we pointed. "Who?" they asked. "What do you see? We see naught!"

"'Tis the witches! All of them! There is Goody Cloyce!"

"Oh, Goody Cloyce, I did not think to see you here," moaned Elizabeth. "Is this a time to receive the sacrament? You scorned to receive it in the meetinghouse. Is *this* a time to receive it?" And covering her eyes as though against the unholy sight, Elizabeth fell to her knees on the church steps. She was immediately joined by the rest of us.

On Monday, April 11, Goody Cloyce stood in the minister's chair, and John Indian, at his own request, was brought in to testify.

By now the problems of little Salem Village were known over a great area. No doubt they had grown apace through the telling and retelling—though they were horrible enough without any exaggeration—and the gravity of Salem's plight had enlisted the efforts of leaders of Massachusetts Bay Colony. At the hearing for Sarah Cloyce it was the deputy governor, Thomas Danforth, who did the questioning.

John Indian stood beside the heavy table, shoulders slouched. There was something furtive in his manner, yet his eyes were bright with an inner excitement as they glanced toward where the nine of us sat. 'Twas as if he knew it would be safer to become an accuser than a possible accused.

Master Danforth opened the hearing calmly, his voice low and sympathetic. "John, who has hurt you?"

When the answer came I was close to swooning. "Goody Proctor first, and then Goody Cloyce."

My heart raced, my ears hummed, I trembled in every limb. Goody Proctor! My Mistress Proctor!

"What did Goody Proctor do to you?"

"She choked me and brought the book."

"How often did she come to torment you?"

"A good many times, she and Goody Cloyce."

"Do you *know* Goody Cloyce and Goody Proctor?"

"Yes. Here is Goody Cloyce."

At this Sarah Cloyce broke in angrily. "When did I hurt thee?"

"A great many times," John Indian said, his eyes avoiding hers.

"Oh, you are a grievous liar!" the woman cried, whereupon she was hushed by Thomas Danforth, who resumed the questioning.

I sat there, disbelieving and distraught, barely able to breathe. The voices seemed to come from some great distance so I barely heard them. Elizabeth Proctor! What would John say? Would he think it was one of us who had accused his wife? Would he think—oh, dear heaven!—would he think 'twas *me*? Could I have fallen into a swoon at that moment as—God help me—I had so often before, I would have done so. My mind seemed to have been wiped clean, and I could only pray that this hearing would soon be over that I might get away to think. To try to think.

A different voice broke through into my consciousness. Mary Walcott was being questioned.

"Mary Walcott, who hurts you?"

My nails dug deep into my palms as I waited for her reply.

"Goody Cloyce," said Mary.

"Did she bring the book?"

"Yes."

Thank God! In the questions and answers that followed there was no mention of Elizabeth Proctor. When Abigail Williams was called I clutched the solid wooden seat beneath me to keep from screaming, for if there was mischief amongst us it centered in Abby. But the names she spoke were those that had been said before—Goody Nurse, Goody Cory, and Goody Cloyce. Not a syllable of Goody Proctor.

I know not what else was said. When the hearing was closed Sarah Cloyce was taken off to prison and I, unable to face either John or Elizabeth Proctor, followed dumbly when the girls repaired to Ingersoll's tavern. I found a small corner settle and huddled there, trying to straighten my thoughts. I was hardly aware when Anne Putnum squeezed in beside me.

"So Goody Proctor has been named," she said.

I could barely speak. "Yes," I whispered.

"That should teach Master Proctor a lesson!"

I stared at her. "What mean you?"

"Surely you must recall, Mary, when Goody Nurse was accused. Your great John Proctor looked upon us and said, 'Hang them. Hang *them!*' You must have heard."

"But—"

"He has called us devils. He has told any who would listen that we are mad, demented!"

"He may be right," I said. "Surely this is not sanity, this that we are doing!"

Anne's pale eyes drilled into mine with a feverish brilliance: "Take care, Mary," she said quietly. "You are one of us. One of the possessed. You dare not falter now. 'Twould go hard with you, I swear it."

"But to name the innocent—"

"Who can say who is innocent? We would have named no one had the ministers and magistrates not insisted that we must. If there is blame, surely it is theirs, not ours."

"But 'twas with us that it all started."

"Aye, as sport, and might have been done with quickly,

had not our elders pressed us for the names of our tormentors."

"Tormentors! None but ourselves torment us!"

"I swear I have seen the shapes of witches! I have seen Goody Good and Goody Osburne and the others. They have come to me, to hurt me—"

"'Tis only in our twisted minds, Anne!" I grasped her arm, shaking it. "We have—have—befogged ourselves in some way that I do not understand! Best it were finished before more harm is done!"

Her thin hand removed my hand from her arm. "It is too late, Mary. And I warn you again. You cannot take yourself from us now. We must dispose of all those who would cry us down, who think us naught but foolish, misguided children. We must have the respect of all the village—respect, and our proper place. Take great care, Mary. Do not undo us. If you should—but I need not say more. You know, now, what we can do!"

With prim little steps she left me and joined Abigail and the others by the great fire. I felt desperate and sick. I was just summoning the courage to leave Ingersoll's when I was drawn out of myself by Anne's voice. She was kneeling by the fire, one arm extended, her finger pointing to one of the smoke-darkened rafters.

"There's Goody Proctor!" she shrieked. "Old witch! I'll have her hang!"

# ELEVEN

WAS IT GOD or the Devil who placed John Proctor alone in his keeping room when I returned? He was sitting at the table, working on a bit of harness that had broken, his head outlined against the late afternoon sun that fell in long slanted shafts through a diamond-paned window. He looked up as I stumbled through the door. I closed it behind me and leaned back against it, too weak to stand alone.

"They have named Mistress Elizabeth," I whispered.

There was utter silence in the room. Even the fire seemed to cease its crackle. His eyes, so blue, locked with mine. After a moment he spoke.

"They?" he said. "*They*? And who, Mary, are 'they'?"

"John Indian first, at the hearing for Goody Cloyce. And later—later—Anne Putnum, at Ingersoll's. Oh, Master Proctor, it was not I! Nor did I join them!"

Suddenly I was weeping as though all the tears of a lifetime came at once. Blindly I ran to him, wanting to touch him, wanting his protection. He pushed his chair back roughly across the wooden floor and rose, catching my wrist and holding me away from him.

"I will try to believe that," he said. "But 'twill not be easy. I have seen the work of the 'possessed.' Stay away from me, Mary. I must speak to my wife."

He left the room and I could hear his step, heavy on the stairs.

When Elizabeth Proctor arrived for her hearing John stood at her side. I write this as if I had seen it, but I did not. I was not there. Instead I stayed at the farmhouse, watching the children, weeping, shaking with fright, praying. But I knew the scene so well! I could see in my mind how Mistress Proctor would look, standing above the assemblage, her figure starting to swell with the new babe. I could see John beside her, his hand most likely close to hers. Though I did not hear what was asked of her, I was later told. And it was all so familiar!

It was Thomas Danforth who questioned her. "Elizabeth Proctor," he said, "you understand whereof you are charged, to be guilty of sundry acts of witchcraft. What say you to it? Speak the truth as you will answer it before God another day."

Silently Elizabeth shook her head.

Turning to Mary Walcott, Danforth asked, "Mary Walcott, doth this woman hurt you?"

And Mary murmured, "I never saw her, so as to be hurt by her."

Danforth faced another one of us. "Mercy Lewis, does she hurt you?"

And Mercy opened her mouth, but was unable to speak.

"Anne Putnum, does she hurt you?"

And Anne stood mute and still.

"Abigail Williams, does she hurt you?"

And Abby thrust her hand into her mouth and bit hard on her own flesh.

Not one of them said a word. The girls were as silent as if dumb. And then Master Danforth turned to John Indian. "John," he said, "does she hurt you?"

And John Indian stood there and replied, "This is the woman that came in her shift and choked me."

John Proctor looked at him with angry scorn in his eyes, but made no move.

"Did she ever bring the book?" asked Danforth.

"Yes, sir."

"What? This woman?"

"Yes, sir."

"Are you sure of it?"

"Yes, sir."

The deputy governor looked soberly at Mistress Proctor. "What do you say to these things?"

I know Elizabeth Proctor's voice would have been clear and soft, but I doubt not there was a quaver in it.

"I take God in heaven to be my witness, that I know nothing of it, no more than the child unborn," she answered.

Had it not been for John Indian, Mistress Proctor might well have walked from that crowded room into the fresh air and made her way home with her husband. But with his accusations, the girls found their tongues and fell into their fits, and all was lost.

"Anne Putnum," asked Danforth again. "Doth this woman hurt you?"

"Yes, sir. A great many times."

"She does not bring the book to you, does she?"

"Yes, sir, often, and saith she hath made her bound girl set her hand to it." Thus Anne punished me!

"Abigail Williams, does this woman hurt you?"

"Yes, sir. Often."

"Does she bring the book to you?"

"Yes."

"What would she have you do with it?"

"She bade me write in it."

From where she stood Mistress Proctor gazed sadly at Abby, shaking her head slightly. Facing her directly, Abby cried out, "Did not you tell me that your bound girl had written?"

And Elizabeth Proctor answered, "Dear child, it is not so. There *is* another judgment, dear child."

And on the instant Abigail and Anne fell into the spasms that I knew so well, and Anne, pulling herself to her knees, shouted, "Look you! There is Goody Proctor upon the beam!"

John Proctor's voice cut across the room. "You look for devils, sirs, there are your devils!" And his strong hand pointed at the row of girls and John Indian.

Abigail clapped her fingers to her arm, holding it tightly. Raising her head, she glared at Master Proctor, and I know how her eyes would have narrowed and glittered.

"Why, he can pinch as well as she!" Abby said. "He is a wizard!"

And from all the girls the cry went up. "A wizard! Goodman Proctor is a wizard!"

Jumping to her feet, Abigail doubled her hand into a fist and drew it back as she moved swiftly toward John. Then, as if to strike him, the fist was thrust forward. But as it neared him the fingers opened loosely, the hand lost its force, and Abby touched his shoulder slowly and lightly, instantly shrinking back.

"Oh, my fingers! My fingers burn! The wizard hath burned my fingers!" And she threw herself to the floor and rocked back and forth, weeping.

At last word came to me that Sarah Cloyce and Elizabeth and John Proctor had been sent to the jail in Boston. At that moment I wished that my life would end.

# TWELVE

THE FIVE CHILDREN of Elizabeth and John Proctor could not be left alone—the youngest was but three years old—and there was no choice but that I stay with them. And so it was that I was in the house when the sheriff came.

It was stated by law that the goods of a witch were to be taken from her, just as her life could be. But it was also stated by law that this could not be done until the witch had been tried and convicted, and in the case of the Proctors, neither had taken place. They had been heard, and were being held until an actual trial took place, but they had not been convicted. But with this particular sheriff, the full extent of the law, which he was pledged to uphold, carried little weight. He arrived one morning early in April with a wagon drawn by two strong horses, and an assistant to help him lift and carry. I stopped him at the door and asked his mission.

"Why, to take the cattle and the household goods and whatever else there may be, to be sure."

"But you cannot!" I said. "The children are here—their parents have been convicted of nothing! You cannot do this!"

He spat into the new grass beside the doorsill and looked

at me. "I figure 'twill take more than one lass, possessed by witches or devils or who knows what, to stop me from doing my duty. Out of the way, girl."

I tried to push the door closed against him, but he was much stronger than I. As the children and I clustered together by the hearth, he rolled the barrel of beer to the door, emptied it on the ground, and threw the barrel into the wagon. Chairs and tables, stools and settles, beds and bedding, nightstands and candlesticks, whatever the two men could lift and move, they took. When he tipped the pot of broth I had set simmering over the fire, dousing most of the small flames, and then took the very pot itself, I screamed.

"But what am I to feed us with?"

"Toad's feet and lizards, for aught I care," was his answer.

As many cattle as he could handle were roped together to the back of the wagon, and at last we watched as they drove away. I put my head in my arms and wept.

There was no scrap of news that did not reach Ingersoll's sooner or later, and generally sooner. When Mistress Sarah Ingersoll heard that the sheriff had taken from the Proctors' house all he could carry, she arrived at the door, laden with foodstuffs and comfort. We fed the children, and then sat together in the doorway, feeling the spring sun on our faces. My tears flowed uncontrollably, and whatever I said came through gulps and sobs, yet I needed to tell it to someone.

"It all started as a sort of sport," I said. "A bit of for-

tune-telling, the reading of our hands—Tituba did that—
and sometimes Betty Parris would trance herself, and then
Abby Williams saw the Devil—at least she said she did—
and it all grew somehow, and when the others said they saw
things, then I thought I did, too, and we all went into takings and screamed. I know not why I could not keep myself
from joining them. And then Reverend Parris and the other
men said we must put names to the shapes we saw. . . ."

On and on I went, spilling it all out to patient Goody Ingersoll, the while she listened and soothed me, sometimes
asking questions.

"Then the girls have not told the truth?"

"'Tis more that they have dissembled than lied, I think.
What they say is not true, but they have come to believe it
is. Like hearing the words of Tommy Richards, who has not
been right in the head since the day he was born, and who
makes as much sense as a gabbling babe! But to him, I believe 'tis true."

"But you yourself, Mary. I have heard you speak when
you were at the tavern. You claimed you saw all manner of
things."

"And so I did, ma'am. My head was so distempered by
all that went on that I must have seen the apparitions of a
hundred persons. But now I think there was naught save my
imagination, and the workings on me of the others, seeing
the same things."

"Abigail Williams says that Goody Proctor brought you
the book, and that you signed it."

"I swear 'tis not true!"

"They are saying now that Satan has made you one of his own to punish the other girls for having named so many of his witches."

"They will say anything, Goody Ingersoll, lest their game be stopped!"

"You think it all a game, then, Mary?"

"I know not what to think. There were times when one of us would call out that she was being pinched by one shape or another, and I could feel the pinches, too. When they claimed they could feel hands at their throats, then I fancied hands were tight on mine. What they did, I did—and my heavenly God, look where it has put us now!"

"'Tis no longer a game, Mary. No longer sport."

"No, ma'am. No longer."

When word reached the girls that I spoke against them and no longer considered myself as one of them, they did what I should have known they would do. They named me a witch. I warrant it was Anne Putnum who first saw my "shape" or felt my fingers at her throat, though it might have been Abby.

In any case, on April 19 I found myself standing on that chair, looking down, as others had, at a sea of faces, and I was sore afraid. As for the girls, there was naught in their eyes but satisfaction. I felt that they would have my blood!

My examination was conducted by John Hathorne and Jonathan Corwin, whom I had watched so many times before. Master Hathorne spoke first.

"Mary Warren," he said, "you stand here charged with sundry acts of witchcraft. What do you say for yourself? Are you guilty or no?"

I, who had raised my voice to cry out against other poor souls who stood where I stood now, could scarce find the voice to speak with. "I am innocent," I whispered.

Hathorne turned to the girls. "Hath she hurt you?" he asked.

I looked at their faces. Each of them stared back at me, but only Elizabeth Hubbard spoke. "Yes," she said. "Mary Warren has hurt me many times." And when I gazed at her in astonishment, she fell into a violent fit.

Now Jonathan Corwin turned to me. "You were, but a short time ago, an afflicted person. Now you are an afflicter. How comes this to pass?"

"I look up to God," I said, "and take it to be a great mercy of God."

"What! Do you take it to be a great mercy to afflict others?"

Before I could open my dry lips to answer, all eight girls I had called friends fell into hysteria. How horrible it was to see! They screeched and whimpered, they bared their teeth, they seemed to be trying to pull hands from their throats. I could feel the spirit of it stealing over me! I began to shake and could feel the old blackness rising round me like a thick cloud, but still I knew the truth and thought that I must tell it, for there was naught to help me now except the truth and I, myself. From somewhere I heard my own voice screaming, "I will speak! Oh, I am sorry for it! Oh, Lord help me! Oh, good Lord, save me! I will tell! I will tell!"

And then the blackness covered me and I felt the hard wood of the chair as I fell, and then strong arms carried me out into the air.

As I gradually came back to myself I could barely remember what I had said. I was only grateful to be away from those faces, beyond hearing of the girls' ravings. At least, I thought in my stupidity, I had told the magistrates I was innocent of their charges. I had said I would tell them all they wanted to know about our "possession." But while I sat there in the soft April air, unable to speak for myself, Anne Putnum had taken my case in her small hands.

"Mary was *trying* to confess to witchcraft, sir. You heard her promising to tell you of how it all came about. But then the shapes of Goody Cory and Goody Proctor fell upon her and choked her until she could not speak. You must have seen them yourself, sir."

"We saw nothing but an afflicted girl."

"But not as we are afflicted, sir. Mary was being set upon by the other two witches so that she might not tell of her own witchcraft. Satan must protect his own just as we must seek them out."

I knew nothing of this. I only wanted to recover from my weakness and explain to the magistrates that I was sorry I had ever allowed myself to be guided and misled by the other girls. They will believe me, I thought. They will believe me because it is true.

I was not summoned back into the meetinghouse. Instead

I was taken across the road to Ingersoll's ordinary, where the two magistrates joined me in a little room that Goody Ingersoll opened for us. That dear woman's eyes seemed to offer me sympathy and strength as she left the three of us alone.

Just being closed in with the two men brought on my trembling again. I sat crouched in my chair, my hands clenched together, trying to keep my poor brain on what was being said to me, so that I might answer correctly.

"Tell us how it is that you are now a tormentor," they said, "for surely those poor children there in the meeting-house were made to suffer by you."

"They brought me to it," I said, my teeth chattering. "I will tell, I will! They did it. They did!"

"They have done naught since you left the room. 'Twas only when you were there before them that they had their fits, as they do whenever they are faced with a witch. As you yourself once did."

"No, no," I moaned. "'Tis not that way! I will tell!"

"Have you signed the Devil's book?" Jonathan Corwin asked.

"No!"

"Have you not touched it?"

"No!"

If ever I had a nightmare, that was it. Each word I spoke they twisted until they would have it that I was a witch confessing, instead of a weak and foolish girl who had helped send innocent folk to prison. Surely Satan was punishing me then, nor could I find the hand of God. The people of

Salem Village would believe what they wanted to believe, and they wanted to believe that the children were naming the witches, and that I was one. I lost all reason. I could but jibber when I wanted to speak. I fell to the floor in tears when I tried to find words to make those men understand my plight. The girls had done their work well.

I was taken to the jail in Salem Village.

# THIRTEEN

AT THE SAME TIME that I was taken to Salem Prison so were others, named, as I was, witch. There was Giles Cory, that bewildered old man; there was Bridget Bishop, and there was Abigail Hobbs. All had been heard on the same day as I, all had been accused, and all had been taken to the village's small jail to await a formal trial.

Goody Bishop's preference for highly colorful dress may have made her unpopular with other Salem females who wore none but muted shades, and the two taverns she ran were so noisy they had brought frowns to many faces. As reasons for naming her a witch they did not seem sufficient.

As for Abigail Hobbs, she did not even live in the village, but in nearby Topsfield, where she alarmed the homeowners by wandering through the woods at night, peering through windows at what her neighbors might be doing, and uttering strange little cries in the moonlight. Even Abigail's mother, Deliverance, spoke of her daughter as a "dafter." But Abigail had relished her hearing in the meetinghouse, and had lost not a moment in admitting that she was, indeed, a witch. She had described unholy meetings held in Samuel Parris's pasture, where she had been one of ten, she claimed, who gathered there regularly. She also lightheartedly insisted that she had committed more than one murder of boys and girls who had angered her, though she could not recall who nor why. In the face of such testimony the magistrates had no choice but to deposit her in Salem Prison, where she was to bide until her trial, though they may well have doubted her story because of its all too fluent eagerness.

So there we were, and in the quiet of the small building we talked together. Except for Abigail, who made little sense at best, we knew we were not witches. It was a comfort to share our feelings, to realize that a trial would prove we were innocent of witchcraft, and that we would be released. When one *knows* one is not guilty, one cannot conceive of anyone else thinking it. After a day or so I felt myself becoming calmer. I chafed at being held prisoner, but without the questions and the accusations, without the misunderstandings and the insistence on guilt, my mind began to move smoothly and I was filled with hope and confidence. It was short-lived.

Although the magistrates and the ministers had been busy with—God help them!—nigh a dozen more accused persons, they would not let me be. They visited me and posed their questions until I trembled and shook from listening to them. So many of them! Samuel Parris and Deodat Lawson, Reverend Noyes and Reverend Hale, Magistrate Hathorne and Magistrate Corwin. Their voices struck against my wits like mallets. They stood around me, their eyes searching me as if to uncover some foul thing.

"Have you signed the Devil's book?" they asked, and I answered, "No." "Have you touched it?" they asked, and I answered, "No." "Has it not been brought before you by Goody Proctor?" they asked, and I answered, "No." And I thought of Anne Putnum and her threats should I try to break away from the group, and I cried out, "She saith she owes me a spite! Avoid her! Avoid Satan, for the name of God, avoid!" And they took it that I spoke of Mistress Elizabeth Proctor, and they beat upon me with their questions until my lips could speak no sense and my body shook, and I was again pitched into the black clouds of madness.

After some hours they would leave me, and just as I would begin to feel my poor brain settling itself into sanity, back they would come with their drumming questions, their accusations, their relentless voices, and their eyes. I tried to answer them sensibly—God Himself knows I tried —but I was so afeared of those men with their long, doubting faces, their urging voices, their power! I sat and wept before them, my face deep in my hands, my heart filled with shame at the harm done to Elizabeth Proctor and John. To save them and to save myself I must speak nothing but clear truth, I told myself, over and over again. Naught but truth!

And thus, when John Hathorne asked me, "When you lived in the Proctors' house, did you ever see such things as poppets? Or great books with strange words within them? Or ointments whose uses you did not know? Or any other such?"

"Poppets?" I asked, confused. "You mean like doll babies?"

"Yes. Like doll babies. Did you see such?"

"Yes. But they were for the children."

"You are sure? You never saw such a thing with, let us say, pins stuck in it, perchance?"

"Sometimes, if Goody Proctor could find no proper cushion in which to keep her pins, for the children would use the little cushions to play with, you know, then she might place her pins in a poppet, to keep them safe. . . ."

"And ointments?" they asked.

And speaking the truth still, I told them, "Aye, many ointments. Goody Proctor knows a score of excellent cures."

"And books? Books with strange words?"

"There were books," I said, "but I had little time to look within them."

And in every case I spoke the truth, and still they pressed at me with their words and askings until, beside myself with confusion and fear and shame, I cried out, "Oh, Mistress Proctor! Hast thou undone me body and soul?"

And they took it as accusation against her, and with satisfaction writ large upon their faces, they left me for that day, and I sank back into the blackness which now I welcomed. But the next day, and the next, and yet the next they came, and whatever I told them was turned and twisted until there seemed no truth in all the world.

And then, the most frightful day of all, they came again.

Again they battered me with their unending questions, repeated over and over, until I felt bruised by their voices. They brought their faces close to mine and their hard eyes pinioned me. "Confess," they said. "Confess to thy witch-craft!" And when I spoke the truth and said I was no witch, they would not accept it, and urged me further, until I cowered there on my stool, my hands clasping my arms, rocking back and forth in anguish, the tears drenching my face, and when they said again, "Confess! Confess thy witchcraft and be free," I could bear no more and screamed at them, "Yes!" Whatever they asked me then, I cried out, "Yes! 'Tis true! Yes!" And they sighed at last, and smiled at their achievement, and patted me, and then they said there was but one thing more and the word *yes* was almost at my lips.

"Tell us that you know John Proctor to be a wizard," they said.

And all I wanted was to be left alone, and in my aching, tormented brain I heard John's voice saying, "Hang them." "They should be whipped," I heard his voice say. "They are devils," I heard his voice say. And last of all, "Stay away from me, Mary!" And his eyes had been as cold as ice and he had given me no comfort.

And the men around me said again, "Confess John Proctor is a wizard, so that your soul will be clean again."

And I heard my own voice rise above theirs as I fell to my knees on the stone floor of the prison. "Yes," I screamed. "Yes! I have felt a shape above me, and when I reached up and pulled it down to me I saw 'twas John Proctor!"

And then I think I must have swooned, for I knew nothing more until the day that followed when they came again, that body of men, and said I had been freed from my sin and could join my friends, those possessed children, Salem's darlings.

And gently, tenderly, they led me from the jail, and I could not speak.

# FOURTEEN

THERE WAS NO PLACE for me to go. John Proctor's house had been closed. His neighbors had taken the children and were caring for them. In any case, after the harm I had done him I had no right to stay there. The Reverend Parris offered to house me, but I did not wish to be in such close company with Abigail Williams. And so it was that I went to Ingersoll's ordinary, and Sarah Ingersoll bade me stay, helping her in exchange for my bed and meals.

During the days in which I had been half out of my mind in Salem Prison the other girls had not been idle. They had thrown name after name to those stern protectors of the village, the magistrates and the ministers, and each name had been caught and repeated until its owner was brought forth and questioned. It was May by then, a soft, beautiful May, with air made heavy by the scent of lilacs, and early green shoots showing through the rich dark earth of farmlands. Some were heard to mumble that listening to witches would put no food on the table, and they proceeded to get to their planting. But in spite of the clear air, the bird song, the warm sun, and fragrant evenings, the girls continued to spend their hours at Ingersoll's, spying their witches sitting on beams or rafters and throwing themselves into their fits.

As much as I tried to keep apart from them by scouring dishes in the kitchen, or drawing pints of ale or cider in the taproom, or whatever else there was for me to do, it was impossible not to be aware of all that went on. I heard them name the parents of "daftie" Abigail Hobbs, her mother, Deliverance, and her father, William. I heard them name a woman called Sarah Wild, and another called Mary Black. I heard them name Mary Esty, the sister of Sarah Cloyce and Rebecca Nurse. And I heard them name old George Jacobs, to whom Sarah Churchill was bound.

Poor Sarah! It may have been fright at the naming of her master, for old Goodman Jacobs was a hard man who had contemptuously referred to us as "bitch witches." It may have been loyalty, or gratitude for his having given her a home. Whatever the reason, at first Sarah Churchill staunchly announced at George Jacobs's hearing that she had no cause to suspect him of being a wizard. Immediately the girls fell into such frenzies as had not been seen in some time. When Sarah rolled her eyes to heaven for strength, the eyes of every girl rolled heavenward also. When she turned her head away, ducking it toward her shoulder to shut their faces from her, every head was twisted sideways. When at last she screamed at them to "stop it!" her words were thrown back at her in a shrieking echo. And thus, because of her seeming influence over the "possessed" girls, Sarah Churchill was herself accused of being a witch.

I knew well how she felt! Weeping, half-swooning, Sarah finally shouted, "Yes!" to whatever was asked her, confessing to anything in order to be released from the torment of questioning. And with that "confession" Sarah, like me, was forgiven and allowed to return to that powerful group of girls.

I was there when Sarah came to Goody Ingersoll that evening and was brought into the kitchen, away from the group who were at their usual antics in the main room of the tavern.

"I must talk to someone, ma'am," Sarah sobbed, "but no one will hear me!"

"I will hear you, child. What is it?"

"There is no truth in what I said of George Jacobs. He is no wizard!"

"Then why said you those things?" Sarah Ingersoll's voice was soft, but firm. "Why belie yourself, thus causing great harm to an innocent man?"

"They kept asking about the book—the Devil's book, ma'am, the same they mention always—and what was there for me to say? For believe me, Goody Ingersoll, if I told Reverend Noyes but once that I had set hand to the book he would believe me, but if I told him one hundred times that I had *not* he would say I lied!" Tears drenched the girl's face, and in sympathy I took her hand.

"She speaks the truth, Goody Ingersoll," I said. "I know. Things now are such that to proclaim oneself innocent is to declare oneself guilty. Only by lies can we be believed. If we say we are witches, 'tis accepted as truth and we are forgiven. If we speak the fact, and deny all devilish doings, we are said to lie and are condemned as witches. All Salem Village has gone mad, I think, Goody Ingersoll! There is no one left to sift the lies from the truth." And I wondered suddenly within myself when I had come to know this. Experience is a hard, but efficient, teacher.

During those dark days my whole life seemed to be a lie. I was viewed by virtually everyone as a confessed witch who had been cleansed of her black powers by that confession, and I was once more regarded as one of the poor possessed children. The same was true of Sarah Churchill. Neither of us wanted more to do with the other girls, not because we lacked all fondness for them, but because we feared them—feared the enormous power in which they exulted. Again it was Anne Putnum who came to me.

At twelve years old Anne looked now like a woman of forty. By nature small and slight, she had become bone-thin. Her face had sharpened and paled; her little hands with their sticklike fingers were nigh transparent. But it was her eyes that frighted me most of all. They had always been wide and pale, but now they seemed glossed over as though the child were half-blind. They held no expression, they simply stared. To have her gaze at me—*through* me—made me want to run and hide, yet there was no escaping her.

"Mary," she said reproachfully one afternoon, stopping me as I tried to whisk past her with a tray of empty tankards. "What hath come over thee? We see little of thee now, and we miss thee. All thy true friends miss thee."

True friends! And yet, save for Goody Ingersoll, what other friends had I, true or not?

"I keep busy here," I said. "I cannot accept Goody Ingersoll's bed and board without working for it."

"But we need you, Mary. Now, when we are doing God's work as best we can, we need the wisdom of those who are older, such as you and Sarah Churchill."

"God's work?" I repeated. "You call this *God's* work?"

"But of course. To see and name those who work against Him—surely that is God's work, which He has set us to do."

My temper flared. "I do not call it God's work to imprison innocent people, old people, such as Rebecca Nurse and Giles Cory. If that be God's work I want no part of it!"

"Have a care, Mary. You admitted to witchcraft and were forgiven. If you are no longer on the Devil's side, then you must be on God's. There is no other choice."

"There must be, or all Salem has gone mad! Think of Goody Esty, Anne! Imprisoned because you—*you*!—accused her! Mary Esty? A gentle woman who never in her life hath hurt a soul, I swear! To accuse her is *God's* work?"

"Oh, mayhap you have not heard," said Anne in her cool, precise little voice. "Goody Esty has been freed."

"What? When?"

"Just yesterday. When many who knew her insisted I might have erred in naming her, I feared lest they be right. Goody Esty was brought before us again, and none of us was sure of her guilt, and so she was set free. You see,

Mary, we try to do our best, and never to harm an innocent person."

With the smallest smile she left me, and I stood like a gawk with my tray of tankards. Had Anne spoken the truth? Had the girls, in fact, allowed one poor soul her freedom? Did I misjudge them? Was it possible that if I were to join with them again I might persuade them to free others? To free John Proctor? Yes, and Elizabeth Proctor, too! If the girls had let Mary Esty go, perchance they were coming to their senses!

And it was true enough. I heard it in the tavern all that day. The woman had gone home to Topsfield and been warmly welcomed by her family and friends, and now there was great hope that her sisters, Sarah Cloyce and Rebecca Nurse, would soon walk freely from prison. And the Proctors, I prayed. Please God, the Proctors!

'Twas but two days later, and the girls were gathered in Ingersoll's ordinary. The wide door stood propped open to let in the sweet May scents, and the fresh spring air seemed to wash the room clean and fill it with hope. I found myself humming as I mopped the tables, swept the floors, and filled the tankards. I could almost believe we had reached the end of the blackness that had shrouded Salem Village all winter. It was then that Mercy Lewis suddenly screamed aloud and fell to the floor, her body twisting oddly.

For a second I stood, waiting for one or another of the girls to join Mercy in what I felt sure was but one of her usual takings, but no girl moved. Kneeling beside her, I took her hand, so burning hot to my touch it seemed to scorch me.

"Mercy!" I said. "What is it?"

"The pain, Mary! Oh, help me! I cannot stand the pain!"

"What pain? Where? Where does it hurt you?"

"My body is on fire! Oh, help me, Mary, help me!"

I turned to look at the girls who stood a little back of us. Their faces wore expressions of such bewilderment that I knew they were as puzzled as I.

"Anne," I said. "We must get Mercy home where your mother can care for her." Dumbly, Anne Putnum nodded. "Mercy, can you stand?" I asked. "Can you walk?"

"I cannot move. Oh, help me! Dear God, someone help me!"

Quickly I rose, snatched a clean napkin, and wrung it out in cool water. "Here," I said, handing it to Anne, "hold this to her face and head. I will find some way to carry her."

Goody Ingersoll took a sturdy blanket from a chest and went in search of some men to carry the girl. Laying the blanket on the floor, the girls and I lifted Mercy enough to slide her onto it, and so stiff was she in every joint she seemed made of wood. I watched from the door as Anne ran on ahead to prepare her mother, and the men, patrons of the tavern, followed with the corners of the blanket in their strong hands.

"Best send your uncle to the Putnums'," I said to Elizabeth Hubbard, Dr. Griggs's niece, "and let me know how Mercy does."

She nodded and hurried away, while I went back to my chores. As I worked I saw many of the tavern patrons wander off to stand outside the Putnums' house, waiting, most like, for another witch to be named. They, and sometimes the girls, kept bringing word back to me.

"She lies sometimes unconscious! At other times she is racked with such agony as we have never seen!"

"She prays the Lord to have mercy on her soul!"

"Dr. Griggs's medications do her no good."

"'Tis not like other times, she speaks hardly at all. Nor screams."

The afternoon turned to evening and the evening darkened into night. My tasks were done, but still I could not go to bed. At last I threw a shawl about my shoulders and walked quickly to the Putnums' house.

The room in which Mercy lay was crowded. In the dim light from the one candle that stood on a table by the bed I could see the shadowed faces of the girls who stood against the walls. Anne Putnum's parents were there, eyes fastened on their young bound girl, and Anne's uncle, Edward Putnum. Dr. Griggs leaned across the bed from time to time, hopelessly spooning drops of medicine into Mercy's mouth. The dusky room seemed filled with waiting.

Suddenly Mercy moved. Her eyes tight closed, she arched her back, her hands rushing to her throat, her head turning heavily from one side to the other on the crumpled pillow. From her dry cracked lips her voice came in a soft moan. "Oh, Lord, let them not kill me quite!"

I saw Anne reach out and take Abby Williams's hand, and

together they moved to the bed, kneeling beside it. Their eyes wide, they stared at Mercy, and then around the room. It was Anne who spoke first.

"'Tis Mary Esty! The shape of Mary Esty!"

Her father, Thomas Putnum, looked up quickly. "Yet you said she was no witch," he said. "She was freed."

"Still, she is here," Abby murmured. "We can see her. Not clearly . . . "

Mary Walcott rose quickly at the back of the room. "She has chains," she whispered. "She is putting chains on Mercy's neck, to choke her!"

"Who, Mary? Who is it?"

"Why, Goody Esty, of course! Oh, Goody Esty, we freed you! Free Mercy now!" And then she stood as if listening, and then spoke again. "But Mercy spoke naught against you."

Thomas Putnum spoke quietly. "What does she say?"

"Oh sir, Goody Esty says that Mercy spoke not against her, but neither did she speak for her. She says Mercy knows she is a witch. She says she cannot let Mercy live to condemn her."

"All this she tells you, Mary?"

"Aye, sir! Oh, Goody Esty, stop! Stop!" Tears streaming down her face, Mary Walcott huddled on a chair, hiding her face in her arms, swaying back and forth in distress.

It was close to midnight, and with every hour Mercy had become weaker. Now Dr. Griggs's hand on her wrist could barely find the throbbing of life. She lay stiff and straight; her jaws seemed locked together. A hushed consultation took place among the adults in the room, and presently Thomas Putnum and his brother Edward left the house to dispatch the constables for Goody Esty.

It seemed hours that we stood there, watching Mercy as sometimes she struggled weakly, and at other times lay as if dead. Somewhere a cock crew, and I saw that the morning sky was beginning to lighten so that from the window trees and rooftops were becoming visible. At that moment Mercy opened her eyes, stared blankly about the room, sighed deeply and, turning upon her side, fell into a comfortable and natural sleep.

Not long after, I heard it was at that same hour of dawn that Mistress Esty was lifted to ride pillion behind one of the constables, and the horses' heads were turned to Salem Prison.

My heart wept with hopelessness. No matter what had happened, nor how it had happened, no witch the girls had named would ever go free.

# FIFTEEN

LIFE WAS A NIGHTMARE to which waking brought no end. The girls gathered constantly at Ingersoll's, where I could not avoid them, much as I tried. But they could not make me join them! My body might be there, but from somewhere I had gained the strength to stand apart from all their displays. From *somewhere*? From thinking of John and Elizabeth Proctor in that stinking jail. Elizabeth must by now be large with child. Was she kept in irons? Many of the women were, I knew. Did she weep? No, Mistress Proctor would not shed useless tears. Her thoughts would be for her husband; her efforts would go toward upholding him. And how they both must hate me! If they were freed, could they ever forgive me? And what matter if they did, since I could never forgive myself.

I went through the motions of each day's living—scrubbing and cleaning, cooking and tending the bar, getting up and going to bed—and nothing touched me. Once I thought, almost with a smile, it was as if I were but the "shape" of Mary Warren, and not the living girl. An empty shape, filled with quiet horror. For still, day after day, new witches were named.

One was Constable John Willard. How often he had
been sent to bring in some poor soul whose name had
rushed from the lips of the young accusers, how often he
had heard the pleas of innocence from frightened prisoners! At last he stood, strong and angry, in the doorway of
the ordinary, his eyes going from face to face of the girls.
And, as John Proctor had done, he spoke unheedingly.

"Hang them," he cried. "They're all witches!"

A few days later a young cousin of Constable Willard's
became suddenly ill. When Dr. Griggs was unable to help
him, Mercy Lewis and Mary Walcott generously offered to
see the boy. It took only a short while, of course, for them
to cry out against Willard. His shape was plain, crushing
the lad to death. When in truth the boy did die, there was
no possible hope for John Willard.

There were Martha Carrier and Mistress Cary. There
were Mary and Philip English. There were Elizabeth How
and Dorcas Hoar. And there was the Reverend George Burroughs.

Abigail Hobbs had been the first to disclose that a pasture belonging to Samuel Parris, though at some distance
from his house, was the gathering place for witches. Tituba
had claimed not to know where she flew upon her stick, but
now it was clear, and the girls made much of it. There was
a horn, they said, that could be heard at midnight on the
witches' Sabbath. No, they had not heard it themselves, for
were they not clean and pure, God's children? The horn
could only be heard by those who worshiped Satan. Its call
would bring the witches together in the pasture, and there,

in whatever evil light the moon shone down, they conducted their own hideous rites, taking their sacrament of blood, and bread as red as what they drank. Anne Putnum had seen them one mild spring night and cried out to her father.

"Oh, dreadful, dreadful!" she moaned. "Here is a minister come! What, are ministers witches too?"

Shocked, Thomas Putnum questioned his young daughter closely. "A minister, Anne? How can you be sure?"

"His clothes! His black clothes! He is small, and there is much black hair upon his head and face, and upon the backs of his hands. Now he takes his stand in front of the others. He preaches to them! To the witches!" Clapping her hands over her ears, she turned away. "I cannot listen!"

"His name, child! What is his name?"

"I know not. I have never seen him before!"

"But we must have his name!"

And Anne, insisting that she spoke to the shape standing there in the pasture, was answered and repeated it to her father.

"He tells me his name is George Burroughs."

'Twas not strange that Anne claimed never to have seen the man before. She had been but a babe of one year when Reverend Burroughs, minister to Salem Village, had left the small town and moved to Maine. But while still in Salem he and his wife had lived for some time with another branch of Anne's family, the John Putnums, and Anne's mother had taken an immediate and strong dislike to

George Burroughs. Mrs. Putnum's dislikes were frequent, strong, and irrational. Had I been more perceptive then I would have realized what I now see clearly—many of the witches named by Anne were people for whom her mother did not have a good word. It was George Burroughs who had first taken a young, orphaned Mercy Lewis into his home, and it was with Anne's parents that he left Mercy when he departed for Maine. But all of that had been ten years ago. Why now did Anne fasten on his name?

It was but a day or so later, before any official action had been taken—for a charge of witchcraft against a minister must be carefully considered lest an error be made—that Abby Williams stopped just outside Ingersoll's, pointing in front of her.

"There he stands," she screamed. "The Reverend Burroughs! He is the little black man! There he stands!"

A patron of the tavern, one Benjamin Hutchinson, was just about to enter for a thirst-quenching pint of cider after working in his fields. He still held his pitchfork, and now in excitement he struck it where Abigail pointed.

"No, no, you have not touched him! He still stands there! Now he has moved—he is there—no, there—" Her finger shifted from one spot to another, and Hutchinson stabbed viciously with his pitchfork, though he could see no target.

"Ah! You have ripped his coat! I heard it tear! But now —oh! Now he follows me!"

Turning in fright, Abby ran into the ordinary, followed

by Goodman Hutchinson. I heard the girl's voice ring out. "Do you see him? 'Tis the Reverend Burroughs! Do you see him?"

There was a time when I would have "seen" him just as clearly as the girls now said they did. But the guilt I felt for my own misdoings had sealed my eyes against all such visions and I was as unseeing now as Benjamin Hutchinson and the other patrons who were gathered in the room. Brave, foolish man, Hutchinson grimly wielded his weapon where Abigail pointed. "There! No, there!" At last the girl cried out, "Ah! There! You have hit him! Now he turns himself into a great gray cat! He backs toward the fire. You see him?"

"I see him! I see him!" It was Mary Walcott. "And here comes the shape of Goody Good."

Anne Putnum, her blank eyes wide, stared into the room. "Goody Good has taken the cat into her arms—she wants to hide it before it is injured again. See? There she goes away with it!" And Anne's raised hand pointed a moving path across the room and out the door, while every eye in the room followed intently. Every eye save mine. Thank God, I could no longer "see"!

Months ago during Tituba's hearing, when she had spoken of the "little black man," she had spoken too of a "tall man from Boston." In their thorough way the magistrates must have pondered on who might fit that description, but surely they had been kept busy with the endless stream of unfortunates who were constantly being named by the afflicted girls. But now a new name had been mentioned, though it is odd to note that the accuser was never identified. The tall man from Boston, it seemed, might well be that doughty sea captain and soldier, he who had fought in wars against the Indians and who had become an admired authority on Indian lore and life, that son of two of Massachusetts's earliest settlers, Captain John Alden, Jr.

Summoned to report to Salem Village, Captain Alden strode into the crowded courtroom one mild May morning, broad hat jauntily on his head, sword at his side. With him was a friend, one Captain Hill. The girls were in their usual place, and already whimpering and moaning over the mischief that Captain Alden, whom they had never actually seen, was doing them.

Magistrates Hathorne and Corwin had been joined today by a good friend of Captain Alden's, Bartholomew Gedney. Now, before any move was made toward the tall, handsome, middle-aged man who had just entered, Hathorne told the girls to identify him. Turning from their seats in the front row they scanned the room, some of them rising in their seats to see better. As their eyes went quickly from one face to another they seemed confused. At last Elizabeth Booth raised an uncertain finger, pointing at Captain Hill.

"There he stands," she said.

A man close to her leaned forward quickly and whispered, and Elizabeth's finger changed its aim.

"Alden! Alden!" she said.

"How do you know it is Alden?" Hathorne asked.

The unguarded surprise was clear on her face. "The man told me so," she said.

Now Susanna Sheldon spoke, her voice shrill. "There stands Alden! A bold fellow who wears his hat before the judges! He sells powder and shot to the Indians and the French, and lies with Indian squaws and has Indian papooses!" Looking rather pleased with herself, Susanna sank back into her seat as John Alden faced her.

"There is not a word of truth in it," he snapped.

Nevertheless, his hat and sword were taken from him— the girls cringing from the sharp pricks they said his sword had been giving them—and John Alden's hearing was begun.

In their usual way the girls twisted and cowered and whimpered, saying the Captain was pinching them, pulling their hair, tweaking at their clothes. He had been instructed not to look upon his accusers, and now, his eyes firmly upon the magistrates, he spoke.

"Just why do your honors suppose I have no better things to do than to come to Salem to afflict these persons that I never knew or saw before?"

"It is not up to you to ask the questions," he was told calmly. "Turn now, and face the children."

It was all so familiar to me! The moment Captain Alden looked at the girls they fell to the floor, writhing and shrieking.

"Set his hand to theirs," Corwin ordered.

An officer of the court held Alden's hand and touched it

to each girl in turn. Immediately they were quiet as the "wizard" drew back into himself the evil he had put upon them. Gazing at them with scorn, Alden shook his head slowly and faced Magistrate Gedney.

"What's the reason *you* don't fall down when I look at you? Can you give me one?"

"Confess and give glory to God," Gedney replied.

"I hope to give glory to God, but not to gratify the Devil. I wonder at God in suffering these creatures to accuse innocent people."

"These creatures, as you call them, are filled with God's spirit."

Captain Alden's icy blue eyes ranged slowly along the row of girls. "Spirit they may be filled with," he said, "but it is a lying spirit!"

John Alden was a strong man, so much like my John Proctor! His strength did him little good now, for he was held to await trial on charges of being a wizard. However, unlike John Proctor, Captain Alden was an important man throughout Massachusetts. Instead of being jailed he was placed under guard in his own home in Boston.

# SIXTEEN

'TWAS THE END of May then, that beautiful month of promise, but not mayhap so beautiful nor so promising to the thirty or more accused witches who lay in various jails awaiting trial. The stories that came from those jails terrified me! Filthy, most of them were, and now overcrowded, since no prison built by God-fearing, dutiful Puritans had ever been expected to hold more than a handful of lawbreakers.

The prisoners for the most part were heavily chained, though that seemed a useless precaution since their shapes were so often still seen by the girls. Their food was of the poorest, and ill-prepared. They were constantly forced to submit to physical examinations of the most debasing kind, the search for any small growth that might answer the description of a "witch's teat." Cruelty had grown among the authorities, whose cool sanity seemed to have deserted them, and two of Martha Carrier's young sons were tied head to heels in an effort to make them accuse their mother. Bravely they resisted until the blood came from their mouths and then they said whatever their torturers wanted to hear. And oh, God help us all, John Proctor's eldest son was chained in the same manner when he visited his parents in prison, and being only human he finally moaned "yes" to everything, and was allowed to take his racked and agonized body safely away. Salem Village and the countryside around it had gone mad, and who is to say where the most guilt lay—with the young accusers, or with the older believers?

No wonder then that the actual trials were longed for, since they promised to end the suffering one way or another. Even though it was well known that a recognized witch would not be permitted to live, those poor souls who filled the jails must have felt that an honest trial, conducted by the clearest, wisest minds in Massachusetts, would prove their innocence. And so all of Salem awaited the opening of the witchcraft trials.

I do believe that the seven men who were selected as judges were chosen as wisely as was possible. Certainly they were aware of what had absorbed all of Massachusetts, but few had been close to the affair. Samuel Sewall, John Richards, Wait Winthrop, and William Sergeant came from Boston. The man named presiding justice, Deputy Governor William Stoughton, was of Dorchester, and Nathaniel Saltonstall came from Haverhill. Only one was a Salem man, the same Bartholomew Gedney who had been present when Captain John Alden was examined. Stephen Sewall, whose Salem Town house still sheltered little Betty Parris, was named clerk of the court, and Thomas Newton was King's Attorney. The two magistrates who had conducted the examinations for so long, Hathorne and Corwin, were at the same task as the girls continued with their "God-given" gift of discovering witches.

The first trial was held on June 2, and Bridget Bishop stood as the accused. Although no longer young, she was a well-featured woman, with brilliant black eyes and a shapely figure. Her liking for such fripperies as scarlet bodices and fancy laces was disapproved of by Salem women, but more serious was the charge that the two taverns she ran were frequented by young people of Salem Town and Beverly, who roused peaceful villagers from sleep with their lusty singing and riotous games of shovel-board. In themselves these complaints might not have been sufficient to condemn her as a witch, but now her trial brought forth more damning stories. Bridget was accused of having a "smooth and flattering manner" toward men, and there were male witnesses aplenty to swear to this. They told of being visited at night by her shape, of spending sleepless hours as she hovered much too close above their beds. They told of how, when they refused to look at or speak to her in their daily lives, pursuing their virtuous ways, she had caused the deaths of children of three of them.

The mother of wild-tongued Abigail Hobbs, Deliverance, who had unwittingly confessed to being a witch and was therefore released, was brought to describe how Goody Bishop had helped to serve the witches' Sabbath in Reverend Parris's pasture. In short, there was none to speak for her, and many willing to speak against her. The jury took scarcely any time to pronounce Bridget Bishop guilty of witchcraft, and on June 10 she was taken to the top of Gallows Hill, where High Sheriff George Corwin hanged her from the sturdy branch of a giant oak tree.

She was the first.

I could tell myself that I had had no part in Bridget Bishop's death, but I knew it was not true. Her hearing had taken place on the same day as mine, and had followed mine so that I was not present to make any display against her. But there was no denying that I was a part of the band of girls who had named her and, though I could not remember distinctly, might well have added my voice to theirs. I had come to know her well in Salem Prison, her and Giles Cory and Abigail Hobbs. Bridget Bishop and I had talked much together, and I had developed a liking for her spirited and friendly ways. To think that I, however unknowingly, had been one of those who sent Bridget to her death brought a shock that nigh undid me.

The girls still made Ingersoll's their meeting place, and though I was believed to be one of them again, within myself I knew that I was with them in body, but not of them in spirit. They knew it too, and it showed in their cold faces. If they felt any touch of guilt for Bridget Bishop's death I could not detect it. If anything, it had made them stronger. They held Salem Village in their hands, and though they were doubted and avoided by a few, they were pampered by the many who watched them in fearsome delight as they went about their godly search for witches and wizards and devils.

It was June 28 before the next trials were opened, and it

was frail Rebecca Nurse who was the first. She said little for herself. Her deafness was such that only shouted questions could reach her, and even those were most likely not clear. She stood quietly, her rheumy eyes fixed on space, unheeding of what went on about her. There were many to speak for her, those who knew of her deep love for her family and her constant readiness to help those in need, but she did not hear these voices. And it may have been as well, for neither, then, did she hear those who spoke against her.

She did not hear Anne Putnum's parents testify that she had killed six children. She did not hear a woman named Sarah Holton blame her for the death of her husband after he had let his hogs get into the Nurses' garden. But most sadly, she did not hear her loyal daughter swear she had seen one Goody Bibber take pins from her own clothing and clasp them in her hands, then cry out that Goody Nurse had pricked her.

The jury, new and inexperienced in such matters as witchcraft, tended to take the accusations of murder as unprovable. They knew that saying so did not make it so, and they were more ready to add their knowledge of her as a reputable person to the testimony that was given in her defense. Accordingly, after but a brief discussion among themselves, the jury returned with the verdict of "not guilty."

My heart sang! There *was* justice in Salem! I would have shouted for joy, knowing that most of those gathered there would join me, but I had no chance. There was a shrill scream from Anne, and then, like a pack of young wolves, the girls opened their throats. Never before had they fallen into howls and shrieks such as these. Never had they twisted their bodies in such terrifying convulsions. The sound beat upon my ears, the dreadful sound of young voices raised in animal-like baying, the sound of young bodies thrashing upon the wooden floor. Dear God! And I had once been part of that!

Chief Justice Stoughton, a cold, solemn man, summoned the spokesman of the jury, Thomas Fisk. Lifting his voice until it could be partially heard above the raging of the girls, he said, "I will not impose upon the jury, but I must ask you if you considered one statement made by the prisoner."

Those words were enough to reach the girls, and gradually their howling ceased. Stoughton paused for complete quiet, and then went on, his words plain now to everyone in the courtroom.

"When Deliverance Hobbs was brought into court to testify, the prisoner turned her head toward her and said, 'What, do you bring her? She is one of us.' Has the jury weighed the implications of this statement?"

Master Fisk, his face bewildered, turned to look upon the jury. Silently, with small shakes of their heads and shrugs of their shoulders, they indicated they had heard no such statement.

"We have no recollection of those words, sir," Fisk murmured.

"Nevertheless, they were spoken by the prisoner," the Chief Justice stated. "And does it not come to you that Rebecca Nurse recognized Goody Hobbs as another witch? One with whom she had shared indecent revels on past occasions? Plainly, that Rebecca Nurse was admitting openly that she herself was a witch?"

"If your honor will permit, the jury will meet again."

"I think that would be wise, Master Fisk."

There was no doubt then. The girls had won, would always win. Sarah Churchill, sitting next me, laid her hand on mine. Neither of us had words.

Rebecca Nurse was found guilty of witchcraft. I do not think she knew what was being said. Mutely she walked to the door between two burly officers, looking smaller and frailer than ever. They took her back to jail.

The rest of those who were tried that day and during the few following days were also found guilty: Elizabeth How, Goody Good, Sarah Wild, and Susanna Martin. All five were hanged on Gallows Hill on the nineteenth day of July, that black year of 1692.

They were buried on the slope of the hill, but somehow —somehow—Goody Nurse's body was moved. 'Twas said her children had quietly taken her home, to lie in her own acres beneath her lilac trees. Somehow no one saw it happen.

# SEVENTEEN

I HAD HEARD that old Goody Osburne had died in jail, quietly, peacefully, just fading away, and I rejoiced. A far better way! And now I heard that Mistress Cary, who had been accused by John Indian with the support of the girls, had been spirited away by her husband, Nathaniel Cary. No one knew how, no one knew where. When his wife had been led away from him after her hearing, Cary had shouted violently, "God will take vengeance! God will deliver us out of the hands of unmerciful men!"

Whether 'twas God who helped Mistress Cary to escape, or her husband with the aid of friends, no one could say. They had gone and could not be found.

And after them, heartened by their success, went Bridget Bishop's stepson, Edward, and his wife, Sarah. Off—away —and who could say where? And then Mary and Philip English. And finally Captain John Alden, Jr. He had been kept under guard in his home, but at last his short patience was exhausted. In some manner he departed one night, arriving in Duxbury to beat upon the door of friends, crying, "The Devil is after me!" He was never seen again in Salem.

Whispers had it that most of these were given protection and sanctuary in New York. Little effort was made to find them, and in truth there was little surprise that escape had been possible. By now there were many in whom doubt about the trials had been raised, many who had had enough of accusations and executions. The guards and jailers themselves may well have felt so. It is of small wonder that they chanced to be absorbed in other duties at convenient times.

It gave me new heart. If Mistress Cary, the younger Bishops, the Englishes, and Captain Alden could gain their freedom, why not the Proctors? They were respected throughout the community, they had friends, they had courage. I prayed. Dear God, how I prayed! Tituba had once said that I held John's life in my hands. I tried desperately now to think how I might save that life. It was hinted that jailers might have been bribed for those earlier escapes, but I had no money for bribery. I considered going to see them, for all prisoners were permitted visitors, and perhaps I could have put the thought of escape in their minds. Yet I could not. Shame and horror at what I had done consumed me, as they do today, and I knew I could not face them. The memory of John's eyes when he had held me off from him, when he had said, "Stay away from me, Mary," was still too clear. And so, with naught else to do, I continued to pray.

Prayer! Prayer can avail you nothing!

On August 5 trials began for Constable John Willard, for Sarah Churchill's aged master, George Jacobs, for Mar-

tha Carrier, for the minister—the "little black man"—
George Burroughs, and for John and Elizabeth Proctor.
Sarah Churchill and I were ushered to seats with the favored band of accusers, and we sat at the far end of the
row, our hands clasped tightly together. I think not once
during the days of the trial did either of us speak. What
was there to say? It had been our own words that had
brought three of those people there.

I know I sat there. I know the trials went on around me.
I know that from time to time the girls were called upon to
give evidence of things they had seen or agonies they had
suffered at the hands of these followers of Satan. I seemed
to hear nothing, to feel nothing, except at one moment
when John Proctor's eyes met mine. Unthinking, I leaned
forward in my chair, my hand lifted toward him, and my
lips, Sarah told me, breathed his name. There was no expression in John's eyes at all. None. After a moment he
turned his head away, and never did he look back.

I know not how many days it lasted. Elizabeth Proctor
was given a stay of execution until her child should be
born. All the rest were condemned to die by hanging.

The road from the jail to Gallows Hill led past Ingersoll's. It was the nineteenth day of August, hot, people said,
though I felt nothing. I stood scouring the counter in the
taproom, my hand moving round and round as if it had a
life of its own. It must have had. There was no other life in
me. The sound of the heavy prison wagons was unmistak-

able, their wheels rumbling on the hard-packed dirt of the road, the horses' hooves clopping slowly. If ever I knew Hell it was at that moment. I laid the scouring cloth neatly below the counter, walked through the taproom, the main room, and the kitchen, and went out the back door of the tavern. Sarah Ingersoll saw me go and said nothing.

In the fields that led away from Salem Village the uncut grass grew tall, brushing thickly against my skirt as I walked. I could feel the sun on my head, but there was no warmth in it. I recall being in a small wood where a stream rilled through. I think I sat beside it for a while, dropping leaves and small twigs into the water and watching them drift away. I remember climbing a hill somewhere and looking down on a small cove of Massachusetts Bay, smelling the fresh scent of the water, watching the sun sparkle on it. I must have walked for most of the day, for there came a moment when I saw the sun was flinging its brilliant orange streamers from low in the west. I turned back toward Ingersoll's.

I walked in as quietly as I had walked out. The taproom was filled, but strangely quiet. A few faces turned toward me and then turned away. There was no sign of the girls. Goody Ingersoll looked at me, made a movement as though to come to me, and then paused.

"Are you all right, Mary?" she asked softly.

"Yes, ma'am," I said.

She hesitated, then took the few steps that brought her to me. She laid a hand on my shoulder, and her face was filled with compassion.

"'Tis said he looked strong, Mary, and was very calm," she said.

I bowed my head. "Thank you," I whispered.

"Go to your room now, Mary. I can manage tonight without you."

"Thank you," I said again.

I closed the door of my room quietly behind me, undressed, brushed my hair, and lay down on the bed. Stretched out on my back, stiff and still, I watched as night moved into every corner of my room. I remembered each word John had ever said to me, the rare sound of his laughter, the touch of his hand. In the darkness I could see his thick, rough hair that I had so often yearned to lay my hand on. I could see the deep blue of his eyes, and the strong width of his shoulders. And then against the darkness my mind saw the outline of Gallows Hill, and a body swinging, swinging, swinging—

Suddenly I was choking with sobs. I pulled the pillow across my face to stifle the crying. I turned and thrust my face hard against the mattress. I drowned in tears that brought no relief, I ached with sobs, I beat my clenched fists against the bed. Then there were arms around me and Sarah Ingersoll pulled me close, rocking back and forth, pressing my head against her shoulder.

"There, child, there," she murmured, and her voice was choked with sorrow too. I reached my hand up to touch her cheek; it was as wet with tears as my own. For a long time we stayed so, she whispering soothing words such as one might use to a babe, rocking me slightly, wiping my face and her own with a corner of the bedclothes. The storm of weeping slowed until there were but a few last shuddering sobs. Goody Ingersoll laid my head gently back on the pillow, smoothing the wet hair away from my face. Leaning forward, she kissed my forehead.

"Sleep now, Mary. Sleep, child. God will help you."

# EIGHTEEN

IT WAS NOT the end, of course. There were further trials in September. I went to none of them; in fact, rarely did I leave the tavern and the strength that Goody Ingersoll gave me, but I heard. I could not help but hear. The girls continued to gather there, and the change in them sickened me. No longer did they see shapes, nor scream, nor cry out names. Instead they sat quietly and modestly, acknowledging their position in the village with grave nods or a few words. For there were many now who felt it only wise to be as friendly as the girls would permit. Their power had been seen, and only fools would choose to doubt it. But their faces! Pale, they were, and hard and cold. Even their skin seemed to have thickened. Their eyes were blank and empty, their hands shook over needlework. The beautiful knitting that Mary Walcott had once done so skillfully was now botched, stitches dropped and hanging. They spoke to me. I answered. We said nothing.

Abigail Hobbs, she who had so eagerly professed herself to be not only a witch but a murderer, was among the first to be tried in September, and with her five others, Rebecca Eames, Dorcas Hoar, Mary Bradbury, and two women from

Andover whom Anne Putnum and Mary Walcott had named, Mary Lacy and Ann Foster. Perhaps they learned from Abigail Hobbs while they awaited trial in jail. In any case, each confessed herself a witch. As witches they were condemned, and as confessed, and therefore supposedly reformed, witches they were reprieved and allowed to go in freedom. Such was justice.

But a little later in the month others did not fare so well. Their names were Alice Parker and Ann Pudeator, Samuel Wardwell and Wilmot Redd, Mary Parker and Margaret Scott. I knew little of any of them. But there were also Martha Cory and Mary Esty—Goody Esty, who had once known that brief taste of freedom before Mercy Lewis's illness pulled her back. All eight of them were hanged on Gallows Hill on the twenty-second of September, and may God have mercy on their souls!

They were the last, or rather let us say they were the last to meet death in that particular way. For there was also Giles Cory, that slow, stubborn, honorable old man, who throughout his trial refused to say a word. He stood as tall in court as his bent back would permit, and remained utterly mute, although he was told what the punishment would be for refusing to answer the questions put to him. Mayhap he no longer cared. He had not been able to help his wife, Martha. Why try to help himself?

He was taken into an open field beside the jail and stretched upon the ground while heavy stones were placed upon his chest in an effort to make him speak. Finally he did.

"More weight," he said. "More weight."

At last the crushed chest stopped that tired, valiant heart.

The sun rises and the sun sets, and nothing changes this. The days go on, becoming weeks and months and years, fifteen years now since it all happened. Gradually Salem's wounds began to heal, though there are many who will suffer always. Elizabeth Proctor left the jail after her baby was born, and no one chose to recall that her execution had been but stayed, not dismissed. Still, as someone who was considered legally dead, she had no rights to her home nor to the possessions that had been taken from it. Friends took her in, for the Proctors had friends in plenty.

The Reverend Parris found that he had not. For months he had protected the girls from the slow shift of opinion against them. As shock invaded Salem Village at the deaths of friends and neighbors and family members, so hatred grew toward the undeniable cause of those deaths, the possessed girls. The villagers remembered too that it was in Samuel Parris's house that all the trouble had started, that his slaves, Tituba and John Indian, had figured largely, that his niece, Abigail Williams, had seemed to lead the girls, that his daughter, Betty, had been sent away to safety. The large family of Rebecca Nurse refused to attend Parris's church services, and as the weeks passed others supported them, until each Sabbath saw more seats empty than filled.

From his pulpit Samuel Parris read a document in which he offered sympathy to those who had suffered "through Satan's wiles," and he prayed that "all may be covered with the mantle of love and may forgive each other heartily." It was not enough.

The Reverend was relieved of his church and departed Salem Village, taking his wife, his daughter, Betty, and Abigail Williams. As they drove away in Samuel Parris's buggy, their household goods piled in a wagon that followed, Abby sat straight on the seat, her narrow eyes downcast, her face expressionless. Beside her Betty looked even smaller, staring blankly ahead with huge unseeing eyes.

Abby and Betty—and Tituba. That was where it all began. Long before the Parris family left the village, Tituba was released from jail into the care of a new master, a weaver with a mind so practical as to have put little faith in Salem's turmoil. The fact that he might be giving a home to a confessed witch seemed to weigh far less with him than Tituba's ability to cook delicious meals and sew an almost invisible seam.

She stopped one day at Ingersoll's soon after she had left the jail, to meet John Indian, who still did much of the heavy work about the ordinary. I watched her as she entered, her back still straight, her white-kerchiefed head high, her eyes calm.

"Good day, Tituba," I said.

She turned and saw me and smiled. "You speak to me, Mary Warren?"

"Of course. Why should I not?"

"There be those who never will. They say that Tituba—"

I interrupted her gently. "There has been too much 'they say,' " I told her. "I no longer listen to what 'they say.' "

Her dark eyes filled with sympathy. "You be a growed woman now, Mary, and a wise one. But the wisdom, it come hard, I think."

"Very hard."

She took one of my hands, her cool slim fingers turning it palm upward. Looking down at it, she said, "Tituba tried to warn you, child. 'Twas all there, right here in your hand. Tituba knowed it was bad, but only God knowed how bad." She closed my hand again, her eyes lifting to mine. "Be you at peace now?"

Suddenly I felt the sting of tears. "At peace?" I asked. "No, Tituba, never at peace again. But I can live."

"That be all any of us can do, Mary," she said, and with a little pat on my hand she went her way.

And the others? After that last hanging on September 22 there were still several unfortunate souls left in prison. Their trials were never held. Instead, Governor Phips, a merciful man with a conscience, and the superior of the cold Chief Justice Stoughton, issued a general release to all who remained in jails. For many it came too late, but because of it a few were spared to live.

And the girls themselves. Or must I say *ourselves*? For surely I cannot escape the blame that I will always feel. In the time that has passed since that nightmare year, Mary Walcott and Elizabeth Booth have married and moved away from Salem. Elizabeth Hubbard lives on in old Dr. Griggs's house, caring for him since the death of his wife, for he is feeble now. Sarah Churchill left the village quietly one day, and I know not where she went. I have never heard of her since. Mercy Lewis and Susanna Sheldon come often to the ordinary. They drink far too much and their voices rise and coarsen, and their eyes blur and stare into space. Who knows what they may be seeing?

Anne Putnum, after the death of her mother, began to suffer what must truly be called "the tortures of the damned." At last she stood before her church and begged for forgiveness and acceptance.

"I desire to be humbled before God," she said. "It was a great delusion of Satan that deceived me in that sad time. I did it not out of any anger, malice, or ill will. And particularly as I was a chief instrument of accusing Goodwife Nurse and her two sisters, I desire to lie in the dust and be humbled for it, in that I was a cause with others of so sad a calamity to them and to their families. I desire to lie in the dust and earnestly beg forgiveness of all those unto whom I have given just cause of sorrow and offense, whose relations were taken away and accused."

Fourteen years had passed before Anne made her plea, and the passage of time dims even great sorrows. She was taken back into her church.

And I. I remain still at Ingersoll's, doing all that I can to assist dear Sarah in her work. I smile, I chat with customers, I see myself slowly aging and care not.

I met Elizabeth Proctor upon the road today. As she always does, she gave me a small, sad smile.

# BIBLIOGRAPHY

Boyer, Paul, and Stephen Nissenbaum. *Salem Possessed: The Social Origins of Witchcraft.* Cambridge, Mass.: Harvard University Press, 1974.

Boyer, Paul, and Stephen Nissenbaum. *The Salem Witchcraft Papers: Verbatim Transcripts.* New York: Da Capo Press, 1977.

Miller, Arthur. *The Crucible; A Play in Four Acts.* New York: Viking Press, 1953.

Petry, Ann. *Tituba of Salem Village.* New York: Thomas Y. Crowell Co., 1964.

Smith, Page. *Daughters of the Promised Land: Women in American History.* Boston: Little, Brown and Co., 1970.

Starkey, Marion L. *Devil in Massachusetts: A Modern Enquiry into the Salem Witch Trials.* New York: Doubleday/Anchor Press, 1969.

Upham, Charles W. *Salem Witchcraft.* New York: Frederick Ungar Publishing Co., 1959.

# ABOUT THE AUTHOR

PATRICIA CLAPP was born in Boston and attended the Columbia University School of Journalism. Her first novel, *Constance: A Story of Early Plymouth,* was a runner-up for the 1969 National Book Award for Children's Literature. Her other books include *I'm Deborah Sampson, King of the Dollhouse, Dr. Elizabeth,* and *Jane-Emily.* Describing herself as primarily a "theatre person," she has worked for forty years with her community theatre and still directs, administrates, and writes most of the plays that are done there for children. Married and the grandmother of ten, Ms. Clapp lives in Upper Montclair, New Jersey.

*Horn Book* gave praise to the author's last historical novel, *I'm Deborah Sampson:* "A fully fictionalized, skillful treatment of the known facts . . . about a descendant of famous New England Puritans. . . . Like the author's honor-winning historical novel *Constance,* the book is engrossing and ably written."